What the critics are saying:

4.5 STAR TOP PICK! "McCray keeps writing one hot cowboy after another... WILDCARD is filled with sensuality, suspense and humor." *~Robin Taylor, Romantic Times BOOKclub*

5 ROSES! "Jess and Trace are a riot. They are funny, sexy, hot, and passionate and the sex is no holds barred." *~ Carolyn, A Romance Review*

"Just when I thought Cheyenne McCray couldn't write a more sexy and charismatic character, she brings us Jess Lawless... Jess Lawless together with author Cheyenne McCray equals a lethal combination with steamy sex scenes, danger, humor and characters that kick-start a reader's heart." *~Tracey West, The Road to Romance*

"This book is hot hot hot. We're not talking about standing next to an open campfire, kind of warm and yummy feeling fire — we're talking a wild, roaring, five alarm fire that will have you looking down at your fingertips for singe marks." *~ Jen Russell, Roundtable Reviews*

D0027202

Wildcard

Cheyenne McCray

ELLORA'S CAVE
ROMANTICA PUBLISHING

An Ellora's Cave Romantica Publication

www.ellorascave.com

Wildcard

ISBN #1419950819
ALL RIGHTS RESERVED.
Wildcard Copyright© 2003 Cheyenne McCray
Cover art by: Darrell King

Electronic book Publication: August, 2003
Trade paperback Publication: December, 2005

Warning:

The following material contains graphic sexual content meant for mature readers. *Wildcard* has been rated *E-rotic* by a minimum of three independent reviewers.

Ellora's Cave Publishing offers three levels of Romantica™ reading entertainment: S (S-ensuous), E (E-rotic), and X (X-treme).

S-*ensuous* love scenes are explicit and leave nothing to the imagination.

E-*rotic* love scenes are explicit, leave nothing to the imagination, and are high in volume per the overall word count. In addition, some E-rated titles might contain fantasy material that some readers find objectionable, such as bondage, submission, same sex encounters, forced seductions, etc. E-rated titles are the most graphic titles we carry; it is common, for instance, for an author to use words such as "fucking", "cock", "pussy", etc., within their work of literature.

X-*treme* titles differ from E-rated titles only in plot premise and storyline execution. Unlike E-rated titles, stories designated with the letter X tend to contain controversial subject matter not for the faint of heart.

Also by Cheyenne McCray:

Wildcard

To Jan G.
My best bud since our college days,
and all that we've gone through together
over the years.

And, um, those research missions? This one's for you!
Love ya, buddy!

Acknowledgment:
As always, thank you to my wonderful
crit partners, Annie & Nelissa.
What would I do without you two?

And thanks to all you Wild Cowboy fans —
the cowboy in the hot tub, and
that cowboy in chaps are for you. *g*

Prologue

Jess Lawless guided the classic turquoise and white '69 Chevy truck up the winding rain-soaked street and into the last remaining parking spot in front of Nicole's Bed-and-Breakfast. The B & B was situated just off Main Street in Old Bisbee, on one of the sloping hills that reminded him of San Francisco.

He shifted into first, cut the engine and the lights, and firmly set the parking brake—he sure as hell didn't want that truck taking a little journey of its own. The old Chevy had been his grandpa's pride and joy, and shortly before he died, the old man had given it to Jess.

He'd promised his cousin Nicole that he'd show up for her Christmas party, but he had an ulterior motive, too. Namely a keen interest in a couple of the folks slated to attend the shindig. He had his suspicions that they might have an idea where he could find that bastard Ryan Forrester. Of course getting the information from them wouldn't be as easy as walking up and asking.

Forrester was a former Cochise County Deputy who'd gone bad. He'd masterminded a cattle rustling ring as a cover for a drug smuggling operation that he'd gotten himself involved with to pay off gambling debts.

And Forrester was now wanted for attempted murder.

DEA Special Agent Jess Lawless intended to be the man who took that bastard down. But first he had to find Forrester, while at the same time figuring out how the hell those drug-running assholes were hiding the merchandise they were slipping across the Arizona-Mexico border.

Just as he reached for the Chevy's door handle, Jess felt the familiar vibration of his miniature high-tech cell phone. It was powerful enough that he felt it from within the hidden pocket in his specially-designed gun holster that had been sewn to the inside of his duster. He reached under the black duster, slipped the phone out from below his firearm, and checked the Caller ID.

It was his partner Diego Santiago, who'd just hired on as a ranch hand at the Bar One. Santiago had recently gone undercover at the ranch to assist Jess in his investigation, and to obtain any inside information on Kev Grand, owner of the Bar One, and others in the area — rancher, lawman, and cowhand alike. The Bar One bordered the Flying M, where Jess worked undercover as ranch foreman.

Button number one on the phone was a direct-connect line to Santiago. One punch and they were connected.

"Lawless," Jess answered in his slow and easy Texan drawl. Jess's and Santiago's cell phones had such sensitive reception that he could hear as clear as day, cows lowing in the background and the chirrup of crickets.

"Trouble at Grand's," Santiago said.

Jess's grip tightened on the phone. "Yeah?"

"Contaminated stock tank. A good fifteen head of cattle are dead."

With a shake of his head, Jess asked, "Poison?"

"Looks that way. Got an inspector coming out."

"All right." Jess glanced through the rain-speckled windshield, to the upper story of Nicole's B & B, and saw a woman's curvaceous silhouette pause in front of the sheer curtains. "Keep me posted, Santiago. I've got some investigating of my own to do."

Chapter One

Tracilynn MacLeod peeked through the bedroom's filmy curtains and stared out into the drenched December evening. Goose bumps pebbled her skin, the colorful glow of Christmas decorations on each of the power poles somehow mesmerizing her. The sight brought back countless memories of her childhood, of celebrating the holidays in the desert. Some not-so-happy times, but she preferred to think about the ones that were joyous, or at least warm.

Below the B & B, the door of a classic old pickup truck swung open, and Trace watched as a man climbed out. In a fluid athletic motion he put on a dark cowboy hat and shut the door of the truck. With his long black duster swirling around his legs, he looked dark and dangerous, like an old west gunslinger who'd come to town to track down his prey.

The man tilted his head up, his face shadowed by the cowboy hat, and for a moment she could have sworn he was looking right at her. It was as though he could see through the curtain and straight through the tiny little dress her friend had talked her into wearing. Trace's heart pounded and her body had an instant reaction, her nipples hardening and her panties growing damp.

She swallowed hard, knowing she needed to back away from the window, to break the electric current that seemed to connect her to the mysterious cowboy, but she couldn't move.

"Trace, are you ready to come downstairs and join the party?" Nicole's voice sliced through that charged connection, snapping Trace's attention away from the man and to her friend.

"Just about." Trace cut her gaze to Nicole who was peeking through the bedroom door. "I need to fix my hair and that should do it."

"Here, let me help." Nicole bustled in, shutting the door behind her.

"Thanks." Trace moved away from the window and to the old-fashioned vanity mirror. She frowned at her reflection while she yanked down on the tiny skirt of the lipstick-red dress. "This is ridiculous," she muttered. The darn thing barely covered her ass, and her nipples poked against the silky material like mini torpedoes. And the neckline plunged halfway to her bellybutton, showing the full curve of her breasts from the inside for cripes sake. "I can't wear this to your Christmas party, Nic."

Trace turned from the mirror to glare at her best friend Nicole and pointed to the three-inch heeled sandals on her feet. "And where did you find these? If you had a better memory, you'd remember I'm a bit of a klutz."

"You're not a klutz. Well, maybe you used to be." Nicole's blue-green eyes glittered mischief. "And I'd say that dress was made for you. Those long legs, cute little butt…"

Trace snorted. "Stop looking at my butt."

"Can't help it." Nicole backed up, propped her hands on her full hips as she checked out Trace's figure. "I just can't get over how much you've changed in the last four years. No more glasses, and you're so…*tiny*. I didn't even recognize you when you first came to the door."

With a self-conscious smile, Trace studied her best friend since her first year at Cochise Community College, and on up through their fourth year at the University of Arizona. Before Trace had taken off for Europe, she and Nicole had been tighter than sisters...certainly closer than Trace had been to her real sister, Dee. Those last few years, anyway.

"It's all still a little weird to me." Trace raked her fingers through her hair as she spoke. "Having IntraLasik performed on my eyes was the best thing I've done for myself." She smiled. "Other than losing those ten dress sizes, that is."

Nicole cocked her head. "So how did you do it? The weight loss, I mean."

"Healthy eating." Trace shrugged. "I've also really gotten into kick-boxing, and all that exercise has made a world of difference for me."

"And what a difference." Nicole grinned. "Can't wait for our old classmates to get a load of you now. They'll flip."

"You'd think I'd be used to it." Trace smoothed her hands over the silky material of the dress and glanced down at her hips. "I've never had hip bones—well, not that I could ever see." She cut her eyes back to Nicole and pointed to her own shoulder. "And look at this. Shoulder bones!"

Nicole laughed and hugged Trace, her friendly embrace and soft baby powder scent bringing back memories of their college days. "I'm so proud of you, Trace." Nicole pulled away and smiled. "As far as I'm concerned, you've always been gorgeous. But now...*wow*. You're a knockout."

"Yeah, right." Trace turned back to the mirror and pushed her strawberry blonde hair on top of her head to see if it would look better up, and frowned at her reflection. The row of gold hoop earrings down her left ear glittered in the room's soft lighting. While she was in England, just to be different and a little quirky, she'd had five piercings done on her right ear, with only two on her left.

Trace sighed. "Dee's always been the beautiful one in the family."

A beauty that Trace had always envied as she was growing up. Dee had always been the prettiest, and certainly the thinnest. Dee had always won all the awards for barrel racing in every rodeo, and had even been a rodeo queen. And of course Dee had always made better grades.

Trace, well, she'd been the quiet one, all of her accomplishments hidden in the shadows. She'd been on the chunky side, with baby fat that turned into teenage fat and then adult fat—

A slap on Trace's ass jarred her from her thoughts. "Hey." She rubbed her stinging butt cheek with one hand and glared at Nicole over her shoulder. "You're not acquiring an ass fetish, are you?"

"No, dork." Shaking her head, Nicole scooped up a gold hairclip from the antique vanity table. "You've got to stop comparing yourself to your sister. Now sit." Nicole placed her hands on Trace's shoulders and firmly pushed her down onto the bench in front of the vanity mirror. "Look at all you've accomplished."

Trace shrugged. "No big deal."

Nicole narrowed her gaze at Trace's reflection. "Graduated with honors from U of A. Hired by Wildgames—only the best software company in the world. Never mind jetting all over Europe and shooting up the corporate ladder. Hell, you practically run Wildgames' Public Relations Department, and you've only been there four years." She gathered Trace's hair into the clip and didn't even stop for a breath. "And don't forget the best part. You're dating a company VP."

Trace knew better than to interrupt Nicole on a rant. The woman barreled along like a boulder rolling downhill when she had a point to make.

"And now you look incredible," Nicole finished as she fluffed the soft cloud of curls left out of the clip. "Like you walked out of *Cosmopolitan*."

Trace couldn't help but smile at her friend's enthusiastic support. "It's funny how confident and successful I've felt since I left home." Her smile faded a bit. "Until my airplane landed in Tucson. Now…I don't know. Time warp. I'm the old Trace instead of the new Trace."

"Close your eyes." Nicole held up the hairspray can.

Trace obeyed and held her breath as the spray hissed and a wet mist surrounded her. When she heard the can clunk on the dresser, she opened her eyes again and saw Nicole's reflection. She had her arms folded, her blue-green gaze focused on Trace in the mirror.

"You know what I see?" Nicole asked.

Trace gave her friend an impish grin as she waved away the lingering smell of melon-scented hairspray. "A redhead in a too-small red dress with no bra?"

"Turn." Nicole didn't even crack a smile as Trace slid around on the polished bench to face her friend.

"Now don't tell me." Trace scrunched her nose as though she was seriously considering Nicole's question. "A redhead with freckles?"

"I see the same Tracilynn MacLeod that I've known and loved." Nicole crouched so that she was eye level with Trace and rested her hands on the bench to either side of Trace's hips. "You've always been a butterfly, you just finally had a chance to come out of your cocoon."

Warmth rushed through Trace and she bit the inside of her lip before saying, "You're wonderful, you know that? You always know the right things to say."

Nicole adjusted the spaghetti strap of Trace's dress, a no-nonsense look on her pretty face. "Hush up and get that tiny ass downstairs. It's time to soar, Ms. Butterfly."

* * * * *

Jess hitched one hip against the bar while he nursed his beer and studied the crowded recreation room of his cousin's bed-and-breakfast. Nicole had thrown one hell of a holiday party, and it looked like everyone in Bisbee had turned out for it.

Nicole was a distant cousin on his mom's side of the family. He'd really just gotten acquainted with her since being on assignment for the DEA in this corner of Arizona. She knew he worked the area, and knew he was undercover, so she never asked questions about his work, which was just as well.

And if she'd get down here and join her own party, she might be able to point out a couple of the folks he'd heard would be here but didn't know by sight. Like that rich rancher's daughter, Kathy Newman, reportedly tight with Forrester at one time. Jess sighed and took another swig of beer. Damn. Guess he'd have to do a little of that mingling crap he hated.

With the practiced eye of a seasoned lawman, he studied the guests, automatically assessing and categorizing each individual as they danced or socialized. He'd bet his Stetson that couple making out in the corner would be trying to find someplace to fuck real soon. That or they'd be doing it right on the dance floor.

A good-looking gray-eyed brunette across the room had been making eyes at Jess, sticking her tits in his direction, her nipples hard and prominent through her thin black dress. No doubt she'd be a willing roll in the hay.

Jess sighed and tipped back his beer bottle for another swallow. He had no interest in women who were that obvious. A little chase was more interesting.

Hell, he didn't know what he really wanted anymore, just that he hadn't found it. Dee MacLeod had piqued his interest before Jake Reynolds had come back, but he'd never acted on it. Not to mention she'd originally been one of his chief suspects in the local trouble he'd been assigned to investigate.

And then there'd been Catie Wilds—a real spitfire— who would have sparked Jess's libido if she hadn't reminded him so much of his younger sister. He had to admit it was a surprise that anyone had been able to tame that wildcat, but Jarrod Savage had somehow managed to, and the more power to him. Hadn't left the sheriff as much time to pursue his former deputy, Ryan Forrester, but Jess supposed he was doing a fair job for a newly-married man.

Jess downed the last of his beer while he watched Jarrod Savage who was by the buffet table, talking to Ann

O'Malley, a sexy cowgirl with brown hair and blue eyes, who owned a ranch just east of Bisbee. He could just imagine Catie kicking Jarrod's ass if she saw him talking to Ann, whether or not he was just being polite or investigating a lead.

The mellow malt flavor of the beer rolled down Jess's throat as he contemplated making a sexual conquest. It had been a little too long for his liking since he'd gotten laid. He'd enjoyed the company of quite a few women, but in the past few years he'd yet to come across one who could keep his attention for more than a night or two of good, hard sex.

Not that it really mattered. Until he brought down that drug ring infiltrating Douglas from Mexico, and until he got his hands around that turncoat bastard Forrester's worthless neck, he was too busy for any kind of involvement. Especially not the serious kind.

That whole cattle bullshit Forrester had arranged had just been a distraction, a sleight of hand, and a little more cash for the asshole. The real scheme involved smuggling drugs in from Mexico using illegal immigrants for mules. And that was where Rick McAllister of the Border Patrol had gotten involved in the investigation, and subsequently called on Jess.

Jess sure would like to know where that weasel Forrester was holed up. The men that Jarrod Savage, Jake Reynolds, and Jess had rounded up had been damn near worthless as far as information on the drug smuggling and Forrester's current hideout.

Gritting his teeth, Jess thumped his empty beer mug on a tray as he glanced at the brunette again. Maybe a good fuck was what he needed to get his head back in order before he headed back to the MacLeod Ranch and his undercover role as foreman. Hell, maybe that brunette would have some information he could fuck out of her.

Just as he pushed himself away from the bar, his cousin walked down the stairs—but it was the woman beside Nicole who captured his attention. Nicole said something that caused the woman to laugh, and her lips curved into a radiant smile that met her beautiful green eyes.

Eyes that seemed vaguely familiar to him. Yet he knew he'd never seen this woman before, and he never forgot a face. Ever.

Jess's sharpened senses took in every detail of the woman and came up with a puzzle. She appeared strong, sexy and confident, yet there was a contradicting air of vulnerability about her.

Intrigued, he watched her stroll into the room, her movements smooth and graceful. Her strawberry blonde hair was piled on top of her head in a sexy just-got-out-of-bed style, and her jade green eyes were big, giving her an innocent look.

Yet the tiny red dress she wore was made for sin. It hugged her figure, showing off her generous breasts, small waist and curvy hips. Definitely a dress designed to drive a man to his knees. And those high heels she was wearing—*damn*.

A vision came to him—having the woman beneath him, sliding between her thighs, filling her pussy with his cock while her desire-filled green eyes focused entirely on him.

Jess's groin tightened and he shifted his position.

Looked like this night might get real interesting.

"I'm going to have to hire a bodyguard just to beat the guys off of you," Nicole said as she and Trace headed down the stairs and into the enormous recreation room of the bed-and-breakfast. "You're a man magnet. I swear every male in this place is watching you." She pointed to the Doberman resting at the foot of the stairs. "Even Killer, my dog. Look at him staring at you—he's in love."

Trace laughed. "More than likely Killer just wants to sink his teeth into these stilts you call shoes," she said, while at the same time trying not to tumble down the staircase. She could just picture herself landing in a heap, this ridiculously tiny red dress up around her waist—now that would certainly get some attention.

Why had she let Nicole talk her into wearing this outfit, anyway? This was more Nicole's wild style than Trace's. The silver backless dress Nicole was wearing hugged her generous figure perfectly, outlining every beautiful curve. And the daring slit on one side went straight up to her hip bone. Nicole carried it off with elegance and style. Unlike Trace, Nicole never tripped or spilled anything.

Nicole greeted guests with a wave and a brilliant smile as they descended. "Too bad you're engaged," she said to Trace.

"I'm not *exactly* engaged." Trace gave a little shrug as they reached the landing. "Harold just hinted, rather strongly, that he plans to ask me when he comes to the States at Christmas."

Guiding Trace to the lavishly spread snack table, Nicole said, "Close enough. And it's a real shame."

Trace looked from the vat of red Christmas punch to the bottles of wine and decided on a white Zinfandel. At least that way if she spilled it on the carpet, it wouldn't stain. She selected a wineglass and cocked an eyebrow at Nicole as she said, "I just told you that a man is going to ask me to marry him. Now why wouldn't you be happy for me?"

"My cousin." Nicole leaned close, and Trace caught her powdery scent. "The man is to die for, and if you were free, I know he'd rock your world."

Laughing, Trace rolled her eyes. "How do you know Harold doesn't rock my world?"

"Uh-huh." Nicole sniffed. "With a name like Harold, he no doubt wears a pocket-protector and horn-rimmed glasses."

Trace had just taken a sip of her wine and just about snorted it out her nose at the image of her boyfriend dressed like a stereotypical nerd. Even though Harold was a devastatingly handsome man, with his reserved personality she could almost see him in that get-up. Her throat burned as she swallowed the wine and rolled her eyes at her friend.

"Let me at least introduce you to Jess." Nicole put her hand on Trace's arm. "He's one gorgeous hunk of cowboy."

"Cowboy?" Trace shook her head so hard it was a wonder her hair didn't tumble out of its clip. "I left that life four years ago. Even if I was free, and even if something ever came of it, I'm not about to settle down in the boonies. That was another life, another girl."

"Mmmm-hmmm." Nicole rolled her eyes. "You can take the cowgirl out of the country—"

"Trace, is that you?" a man's voice cut in, and Trace looked up to see Rick McAllister, one of the nicest as well as one of the most drop-dead gorgeous cowboys she'd ever known. At over six feet with that chestnut brown hair mussed all over his head, he looked like he'd just come in from a long trail ride. Sexy bastard.

"Rick!" Trace reached up and gave him a quick one-armed hug, being careful not to spill her wine. "Dang but it's good to see you."

"Well, hell. I hardly recognized you." He tweaked a tendril of Trace's hair and gave her his easy grin. "Probably wouldn't have if Nicole here hadn't told me you were coming. You're all grown up now."

Trace felt heat creep up her neck and she shook her head. "Thanks, big guy. You don't look so bad yourself." And he didn't. The tall, well-built man was a good eight years older than her, but she'd sure had a crush on him back when she was a teenager, until he'd gotten married. He'd always been more like a teasing older brother, and she'd come to appreciate him as a good friend. It had been a real shame when his wife was killed in that car accident, leaving him a widower and a single parent.

The faint ringing sound met her ears over the Christmas music. Rick gave Nicole and Trace a sheepish grin as he dug the phone out of his pocket and checked the caller ID. "Sorry, ladies. I'm on call and I've got to take this."

"No problem." Trace smiled and waved him off. "We'll do some more catching up later."

Rick nodded and put the phone to his ear as he headed up the stairs, probably to someplace where it was a little more quiet.

"You know that Rick's an intelligence agent with the Border Patrol, don't you?" Nicole's smile turned into a frown as she started to add, "He's here with—" she stopped as the caterer rushed up and interrupted, telling Nicole she was urgently needed upstairs in the kitchen.

"All right, all right." Nicole sighed and waved the caterer off. "Be right there." She turned to Trace. "Think you can fight off all the men while I go handle this mini crisis?"

"Sure." Trace laughed and raised her wine glass. "I'll do my best to stay out of trouble." Her gaze cut to Killer. "And I've got my buddy right here."

When Nicole left, Trace lifted the goblet to her lips and let her gaze drift over the party guests. It had been good to see Rick, as well as other old friends. Her thoughts turned to her first days back in the U.S., when she'd stayed a few days with another good friend, Lani Stanton. Two years ago, Lani had interviewed Trace about Wildgames, and they'd hit it right off. Lani was a journalist with a popular San Francisco magazine, but she was going through one hell of a messy divorce. Her ex-husband was a cheating bastard. Damn but Lani needed a good man.

Holiday music and laughter filled the room, and Trace smiled as she watched couples dancing to a country-western tune. The room glittered with all the women dressed in brilliant sequined dresses and from the hundreds of Christmas lights and decorations.

Scents of pine, cinnamon, and hot wine punch perfumed the air, along with the smell of burning mesquite wood in the fire blazing in the corner hearth. Sounds, sights, and smells of holidays that reminded Trace of growing up in Arizona, and made her feel like she was home.

Home...

No. Home was wherever Wildgames sent her. And home would be with Harold once he got around to asking her.

That was what she wanted, wasn't it? To marry Harold and continue rocketing to the top of the career ladder? They'd be good together, a match made in Wildgames Heaven.

Then why did the thought of living with Harold for the rest of her life make her feel trapped?

Jitters. Fear of commitment. That was it.

Hair prickled at Trace's nape, as though she was being watched, and a slight shiver skittered down her spine. Slowly she pivoted and came to an abrupt stop. She caught her breath at the sight of the most rugged, most handsome cowboy she'd ever had the pleasure of viewing.

He'd been standing directly behind her, inches away.

Instinctively she took a step back, but in a quick movement he caught her wrist, drawing her closer to him. Her flesh burned where he held her, and her mind went entirely blank.

The man's smile was so carnal that Trace's knees almost gave out. And those blue eyes—God, the way he was looking at her made her feel like he was making love to her right on the spot.

She clutched her wine glass between them as she tried to pull her wrist out of his iron grasp. "I—let go."

The man shook his head, the look in his eyes possessive and untamed. "No, sugar," he murmured, his sensual Texan drawl flowing over her. "You're not going anywhere."

Chapter Two

Sensual heat scorched Trace in a rush. It shot up her thighs and waist, straight to her breasts, and on up to the roots of her hair. He had to be the one she'd seen getting out of the truck earlier. Even without the cowboy hat and duster, he seemed just as dark and dangerous.

Dang, the man was tall. And sexy. He had a strong, angular jaw line shadowed by dark stubble, and the most intense gaze that refused to let her go. And God but he smelled good. Like spicy aftershave, the clean scent of soap, and a hint of malt beer.

Moisture flooded Trace's pussy and her nipples grew taut against the delicate fabric of her dress. The way the man was looking at her, she could just imagine his touch, his mouth —

Hold on. Who the heck did he think he was, telling her she wasn't going anywhere?

Yet she couldn't speak. Couldn't move.

Like a deer trapped by headlights…only what had captured her was a pair of wicked blue eyes and a steel vice grip on her wrist.

The man pried the wine glass from her hand and set it on a table beside them. "What's your name, sugar?"

Trace swallowed and mustered a defiant look. "Well, it's not sugar." Her voice came out sounding small and hesitant, and she forced herself to put some muscle into her tone. "Let me go —"

"Name's Jess Lawless." His firm mouth curved into a sensual smile that met his eyes, and she thought for sure her knees were going to just up and give out on her. "It's most definitely my pleasure to meet you...*sugar*," he drawled, sounding every bit as lawless as his name.

Oh. My. God. Trace MacLeod had *never* come across a man that she wanted to slap then jump the moment she'd met him.

Uh...uh...uh... Take me now, I'm yours.

Okay, she'd set a new record. She'd become a complete and total idiot in less than two minutes.

The man — *Jess* — placed a possessive palm on her waist and took her other hand in his. Before she'd gathered her thoughts, what few she had left, Jess drew her into the crowd of people dancing at the center of the room. "Do you two step?" he asked, even as he led her.

"Uh, yeah." *Brilliant, Trace.* "It's, ah, been awhile." She glanced down at their feet as they moved, and promptly imbedded her three-inch spiked heel into the leather toe of his boot, bringing them to a halt. Her gaze shot to his and to his credit he didn't even flinch. "A really *long* while."

He grinned, a dimple appearing in one cheek, and she instantly became a dithering idiot. Again.

A-duh-duh-duh.

"Well, then," he murmured, moving his mouth close to her ear, "we'll just have to keep at it 'til it all comes back to you. All right?"

"O—" Trace shivered and almost moaned at the feel of his warm breath along her cheek. "Okay."

And can I have your babies, too?

What the heck was the matter with her, she wondered as Jess drew her smoothly into the throng of dancers. Sure, she'd gone ga-ga over guys before — when she was a *teenager* for goodness sake. And those had been the ones in *Teen People* and *The Rolling Stone*. The adorable and unobtainable.

But this was a *man*. And God what a man. Certainly just as unobtainable as her childhood crushes, only now because she was spoken for. More or less.

Er, good ol' whatshisname…

Her pulse rate zoomed past the legal speed limit as they two-stepped to a country-western tune that had been popular back when she'd lived on the Flying M, the MacLeod Ranch. Funny how she could still remember all the words. Yet right now she had a hard time remembering what her *almost* fiancé looked like. All she could picture in her mind was this sexy hunk of cowboy whose mere presence had fried all the circuits to her brain.

Cowboy. Jeez! She didn't do cowboys. Well, not to mention she shouldn't be doing *anyone* but the man she'd been with for the last couple of years.

"Are you going to tell me your name?" Jess's baritone rumbled as the tune came to an end and a much slower song started. "Or am I gonna just have to keep calling you sugar?"

Uh…

Trace's whole body went on high alert as he brought her into his embrace for the slow dance. She placed her hands lightly on his shoulders — like she was afraid to touch him. His jean clad hips moved so close to hers that she felt the brush of denim through her silky skirt. She gulped and her gaze shot up to his. That couldn't be his...he couldn't be...it had to be her imagination. He wasn't *aroused,* was he?

Amusement glittered in Jess's blue eyes as he guided her in a slow and easy turn to the music. "Did you drop your voice into that incredible cleavage?" he murmured.

Trace blinked and then smiled. "Now that's one I haven't heard before."

"Well, what do you know?" He gave her that sexy grin again. "The beautiful woman speaks."

Beautiful. She-yeah.

"I—I'm Tracilynn." Trace gave the name she'd gone by since she'd graduated from college, her given name. The only people who called her Trace were those she knew B.E...before Europe.

"Nice." Jess rested one hand on her hip, but she didn't know if he was referring to her name or her body. His palm felt so hot that it was like he had it pressed to her bare skin, rather than against her dress. "Where have I seen you before, Tracilynn? You're not from 'round here, are you?"

She caught her breath as he twirled her to the song, and he somehow managed to bring her body even closer to his. "I used to live in this area, ages ago. I'm visiting."

"Very sexy." Jess brought one hand to her left ear and lightly ran his thumb down the row of earrings. His expression turned thoughtful. "Your eyes...I never forget a woman's eyes. Hell, I've never forgotten a face. So why are you so familiar, yet I can't place you?"

"We've definitely never met." Trace managed a smile. "I'd remember you."

"Yeah?" He moved away from her and took her hand, his palm hard and calloused against her softer skin. "And why's that?"

With a start Trace realized Jess was drawing her through the open doors of the sunroom. "I really should get back to Nicole," she said, her words rushed and her heart beating furiously as he led her toward the Christmas tree in the corner. "She'll wonder where I am."

Jess's cock strained against his jeans as he brought Tracilynn to a stop beside the decorated tree. Lights twinkled, the soft glow playing upon her delicate features and reflecting in her eyes. He took both her hands in his, resisting the urge to grab her hips and press himself tight against her, letting her feel how badly he wanted to be inside her. He wanted to dispense with the time it would take to get to know this beautiful woman, and get her straight into his bed.

But everything about her told him he'd have to take things a lot slower than he'd like to.

Damn.

"Really, I should get back." Tracilynn avoided his gaze, looking instead toward the rec room where they'd come from.

Jess released one of her hands and caught her chin, forcing her to look at him. Her soft peaches and cream scent eased through his senses. "What are you afraid of?"

She licked her lips, her eyes focused on his. "You," she whispered.

The corner of his mouth turned up. "Now why would I scare you?"

"I—I shouldn't be here." She pulled against his hold, but he held on and raised her hand to his chest.

He pressed her palm against his shirt and rubbed his thumb over her fingers. "No ring." He frowned as he studied her jade green eyes. "You're not married are you?"

"No." She swallowed, her throat visibly working. "But I'm in a long term relationship. Two years now."

The freight train of jealousy that slammed into Jess took him completely by surprise. "Where's your boyfriend?" he asked in a tone that was too calm for the fury churning his gut at the thought of another man with a claim on this woman.

"England." She brought her other hand up to his chest and pressed, as though trying to push him away. But the feel of her palms through his shirt only made him want her more. "He'll be here shortly before Christmas."

Nope. Wasn't happening. No way in hell was Jess letting another man have this woman. If she'd been married, he would have walked away, no matter the bitter regret that would have chapped his ass. But as far as he was concerned, if the man hadn't staked his claim with a ring and a wedding vow, then the bastard wasn't man enough to keep her.

But he had to make sure.

Jess gritted his teeth. "Engaged?"

"Well, no." A fine blush tinted her cheeks. "But he hinted that he's planning to ask me at Christmas."

He released his hold on her fingers and slid his palm onto her hip at the same time he cupped the back of her head with his other hand. "If the man hasn't had the balls to make you his by now, then he doesn't deserve you."

Trace's entire body vibrated, her skin alive in a way that she'd never felt before with — with, er…

Jess brought his face closer to hers, so close she could feel the warmth of his breath on her lips and she could almost imagine how he would taste. His spicy scent saturated her senses, his male presence hard and solid. Everything about him was virile and sexy, dark and dangerous. Definitely dangerous, and definitely not part of the carefully arranged hand Trace planned to play out, meticulously and cleanly, to win the stakes she'd set her sights on years ago. Good job, nice home, stable family a million miles away from desert sands and faithless cowboys—a man like this definitely wasn't part of the draw she needed. No, he was…a wildcard. An unexpected, unpredictable wildcard who could win the game's hand instantly—or wreck it forever.

He was waiting. Waiting for her to tell him no. But all she could think about was how badly she wanted him to kiss her.

No, Trace. You can't do this.

Just one kiss. One little kiss.

Jess made a noise like the rumble of a bull, and a whimper slipped from Trace. A sound of longing and desire.

His mouth crushed hers, his lips firm and possessive. She opened up to him, but he didn't slide his tongue into her mouth. Instead he nipped at her lower lip, small, untamed bites that made her burn in a way she'd never imagined.

Trace moaned and clenched her hands in his shirt as she reached up, begging for more. Part of her couldn't believe what she was doing, couldn't believe what he was doing to her. And a part of her didn't give a darn. She just didn't want it to end.

Jess separated his mouth from hers, but kept his lips close to hers. "I've got to taste you, sugar. All of you."

Omigod. By the tone of his voice and the look in his eyes, he didn't just mean a kiss. He meant every part of her body. Her pussy flamed at the thought of his face between her thighs, his tongue licking her clit.

Oh, God. What was she doing? She didn't even know Jess—she'd just met him what, twenty minutes ago? And now here she was, making out with him like a teenager. A really horny teenager at that.

What about her plans, the man she thought she was going to marry?

She gripped his shirt so tightly her knuckles ached. "Jess, I—"

He cut her off with another hard kiss. Only this time he plunged his tongue into her mouth, demanding and insistent.

Everything melted away. All thoughts of anything outside the feel of his stubble chafing her skin, the taste of him…a heady male flavor combined with a hint of malt beer.

Small purring sounds echoed in Trace's ears, and she realized it was her—a low "*Mmmmmm,*" rose up within her, like she was sampling the finest of chocolates and she couldn't get enough.

And right then she knew the kiss would *never* be enough. If she didn't put some distance between herself and this man right now, she'd never be able to walk away from him.

She tore her mouth from his, her breathing hard and uneven. Jess's chest rose and fell beneath her hands, and she knew he was as deeply aroused as she was. Not to mention that log he had pressed up against her belly. Good lord but the man had a huge cock.

"I, ah." Trace unclenched her hands, releasing his shirt, her knuckles aching with the sudden flow of blood. "I need to use the ladies room."

Jess ran the back of his hand along her cheek and smiled, his blue eyes dark with sensuality. "I'll get you something at the bar."

"Rum and coke would be great." The conversation seemed inane considering the kiss they'd just shared and the wild lust pulsing between them in tangible waves. Impulsively she reached up and lightly kissed him. "I'll be right back."

She slipped away, refusing to look over her shoulder at him one last time, her lips still tingling and her clit still throbbing. As she entered the rec room, she suddenly realized how she must look—her lipstick kissed off, her mouth red from the scrape of his stubble, her lips swollen from his kisses and bites.

He'd *bitten* her for cripes sake.

In her state of total-freak-out, she almost ran into another woman. Her gaze shot up to meet the brunette's furious ice-gray eyes, and the apology died in Trace's throat. "Kathy Newman?" Trace said almost reflexively.

"Yeah." The woman's frown deepened. "Who the hell are you?"

"Excuse me." Trace dodged past the person that she'd once considered her worst enemy in high school. Kathy Newman, the vivacious beauty who had been one of the most popular girls in school.

And the bitch who'd considered it her mission to make Trace's life miserable all four years of high school, and even on into college. She couldn't even take satisfaction in the knowledge that Kathy hadn't recognized her.

No. If Kathy found out who Trace was...*crap*. The woman would no doubt make sure Harold found out Trace had been kissing another man.

The irony in the fact that she'd finally remembered Harold's name almost made her burst into hysterical laughter.

Her face burned as she blindly rushed through the crowd. She stumbled over Killer, but regained her balance and hurried up the stairs.

She had to get out of here, had to get to the ranch, and *now*.

Jess fisted his hands at his sides, lust raging through his body. He watched Tracilynn as she left, a gentle sway to her hips and a little wobble to her walk, like she wasn't entirely used to wearing shoes with heels the size of nail heads.

The corner of his mouth quirked into a smile. He could just picture those ankles around his neck as he slid into her...*damn*.

As he started to head to the bar to order their drinks, he noticed Tracilynn had bumped into the brunette with the big tits, the same one who'd been making eyes at Jess earlier—and the brunette looked pissed, like she'd just swallowed an ant hill.

Jess heard Tracilynn say, "Kathy Newman?" in a surprised tone, and he moved his gaze to the brunette.

So that was Kathy Newman, who was on Jess's short list of people to question in the next few days. Tonight would have been perfect, but not now. At the moment, he had a redhead to deal with, and fast. He cut his gaze back to Tracilynn, but a moment later, she turned and slipped into the crowd, vanishing from his sight.

Right then his gut told him that she didn't intend to come back.

He'd see about that.

The way she'd kissed him, the way she had trembled in his arms, her passionate purr...all had made it clear as an Arizona sky that she wanted him as badly as he wanted her. Problem was she didn't know how to handle those desires.

He was just the man to teach her.

Several inches taller than most of the folks at the party, Jess searched the crowd for the petite strawberry blonde, and spotted her at the top of the stairs just before she disappeared from view. Damn she was fast. He started after her, only to find Big Tits Newman blocking his path.

"Excuse me, ma'am," he said with a nod as he tried to sidestep her.

She placed one hand on his biceps and deliberately moved in his way, her perfume as brazen as she was. "I'm Kathy."

Even though the woman was keeping Jess from going after Tracilynn, his upbringing and professional instincts kept him from being outright rude. His mama had raised him to always be polite to a lady. Besides, he still needed as much information as he could get on Forrester — later.

"A pleasure." He nodded and tried to move, but her hand tightened.

"Care to dance, cowboy?" she asked as she brushed her breasts against his chest.

"I'd be obliged if you'd save a dance for me later." He gave her another slight nod and a tight smile. Before Kathy Newman could respond, he took her by the shoulders and gently removed her from his path.

Well, gently enough.

Jess barely heard Kathy's gasp of annoyance above the Christmas music as he walked away.

In a few strides he made it to the stairs and took them by threes. When he reached the B & B's front room that served as the lobby, he saw Nicole standing in front of the registration desk with a slip of paper in her hand.

"What the—" she said as her gaze cut to the desk clerk. "This is it? All she left?"

Jess didn't stop. He headed straight to the front door and yanked it open.

December's chill air rushed in, but outside all he could see were cars parked up and down Old Bisbee's Main Street. The rain-soaked blacktop reflected red, orange, blue, and green Christmas lights strung down the silent street—but nothing else. Not even a pair of taillights.

Ah, hell.

The click of Nicole's heels against the tile and her powdery perfume alerted Jess to her presence, even before she spoke. "You have something to do with her up and leaving, don't you?"

He shut the door a little too hard as he clenched his jaw and pivoted to face his cousin. "Where'd she go?"

"Her sister's." Nicole shook the note at Jess. "I wanted her to meet you, but I sure as all get out didn't think you'd go and scare her off like this."

Jess snatched the note from Nicole's hand.

Left for Dee's. I'll call. T.M.

"Dee…" His gaze shot up to meet Nicole's furious expression as it finally hit him. Where he'd seen Tracilynn's eyes before. Eyes that had been hidden behind glasses in pictures taken years ago. Photos he'd seen countless times at the MacLeod Ranch. Eyes that had captured his attention the first time he'd seen them. Had made him wonder about the girl…the woman.

Shit.

"Trace MacLeod." He shook his head. Some intelligence agent he was. "Dee's younger sister."

"What would you want with that heifer?" came a woman's voice from beside them. "Last I heard she was in England."

Both Jess's and Nicole's attention snapped to Kathy Newman. The woman had one hand on her hip as she tossed her dark hair over her shoulder.

Jess narrowed his eyes, but Nicole laid into the woman. "I don't care if your daddy is running for congress. I wouldn't give a flying fuck if he was the President of the United States," Nicole said with fury in her voice. "If you *ever* talk about my best friend like that again, I'll kick your ass from here to Texas. You hear me?"

"That was Trace MacLeod?" Recognition dawned in Kathy's eyes, but her tone remained cool as she glanced from Nicole to Jess. "The slut in the red dress?"

"You bitch." Nicole stepped forward, her fist raised, but Jess caught her by the shoulders and held her back. "Let me at her, damn it!"

"Not worth it," he responded in a controlled voice, his gaze fixed on Kathy Newman. *Too hell with information.* "She's definitely not worth it."

The woman smirked and turned on her heel, heading to the B & B's front desk. "Get my purse and jacket," she ordered the pony-tailed hippie behind the counter. "I've got better places to be."

"You're not welcome here." Nicole strained to get away from Jess. "If you hadn't come with Rick McAllister, I'd never have let you through the front door."

McAllister. Thank God. Jess let out a short breath. McAllister'd likely be able to get the skinny on Forrester from Big Tits, even though she'd sooner spit than talk to Jess now. Good ol' Rick sure needed help with his taste in women, though.

"Well, Nicole, you still have the hots for Rick, I see." Kathy Newman took her belongings from the clerk and walked to the front door, saving a particularly spiteful look for Jess's cousin. "He'd never go for a fat ass like you, sweetie."

"Let me punch her now." Nicole's face was red, and she struggled like a hellcat against his hold. "Come on, Jess."

Kathy paused at the front door, her gaze raking Jess from head to toe. "What a waste," she said before heading out the door in a swirl of too-sweet perfume.

When the door slammed shut behind the bitch, Jess turned Nicole around and said, "Now tell me about Trace MacLeod."

Chapter Three

Trace gripped the steering wheel of the sleek rented Mustang while she headed into the night and out of Bisbee on the hour drive to the Flying M. Fortunately she'd packed her luggage in the trunk before the party, so all she'd had to do was grab her purse and coat from the desk clerk and scribble a quick note to Nicole before she'd fled.

Blacktop and yellow highway markings scrolled by her headlights, glittering from the recent rains. Her thoughts whorled — she couldn't believe she'd just kissed another man. Should she be upfront and tell Harold? Or was it better left unsaid? A one time mistake that wouldn't be repeated.

Yet her stomach flipped and her pussy grew wetter as she remembered every moment in Jess's presence. The way he'd staked his claim on her, as though he intended to make her his. The way he'd brought his mouth to hers and paused, his breath warm on her lips, just waiting to see if she'd refuse him.

And oh, God. The way he kissed. The way fire had seared every part of her body, like flames burning just beneath her skin. She'd never felt such intensity with any other man. She was so horny now she could almost scream. If she hadn't slipped away, would she have ended up in bed with him?

Would she have cheated on Harold?

Her face grew hotter, but she couldn't tell if it was embarrassment at what she'd done...or the heat of desire from imagining what it would be like to make love to Jess.

Trace flipped on the radio in an effort to get her mind on something else. The rich voice of the man singing a popular country western tune only reminded her of Jess's deep baritone.

She tried to turn her thoughts to the deserted country highway, tried to get the cowboy out of her mind, but it was impossible. Instead, her nipples grew tighter against the silk dress, and her clit felt swollen and raw as her thong panties rubbed against her folds.

Considering the chilly desert night, she was burning hot.

Jeez. She couldn't get to Dee's looking like this—decked out in this tiny little outfit, looking like she'd just made out with a guy. What was she thinking?

Trace kept her eyes open for a dirt road and pulled the Mustang onto the first available one she spotted. Good thing this was such a rural area. She could make a quick change and get back on the road.

After she made sure she was well off the highway, Trace parked the car and turned off the ignition, but left the radio on. The blue glow from the dashboard was the only light in the car, but outside the moon slid from behind a scrap of moody clouds and washed the desert with its silvery radiance.

She leaned her head against the cool glass of the side window as she looked up at the incredible display above her, stars glittering in patches where clouds had retreated. She'd forgotten how bright the stars were out here in the country, far from any towns. It was beautiful. What would it be like to make love to Jess under these stars?

No, *Harold*. She meant what would it be like to make love to *Harold*.

Yeah, right.

With a groan, Trace reached between the bucket seats to grab her duffle out of the back. From years of travel experience, she always kept a quick change of casual clothes in a carry-on bag, along with basic necessities, just in case her luggage was lost at the airport or stolen from the trunk of her car.

Her dress pulled against her breasts as she stretched her hand toward where the duffle rested on the floorboard, and one nipple popped free. It felt cool and erotic rubbing over the leather seat of the Mustang as she reached for her bag. Her thong slid into her folds, pressing harder against her clit.

Maybe what she needed was a good orgasm. It had been at least a couple of weeks or longer since she'd had sex with Harold. He'd been tired from work one week, and the next had been an inconvenient time of the month for her, and then she'd left for the States a few days ago.

Trace settled back in her seat, leaving the duffle where it rested. She brought her hands up to her breasts and cupped the bare nipple and the one still covered by the thin material of her dress. Instead of the one man she'd had sex with for the past two years, she could only visualize Jess. Could only imagine his hands caressing her, flicking his thumbs over her nipples.

She eased her breasts free of the plunging neckline, her nipples beading even tighter in the cool air. Her pulse picked up at the thought of Jess's mouth on her nipples, licking and sucking, and *biting* her the same way he'd kissed her.

Slipping one hand between her thighs, Trace ran her fingertips over the soaked crotch of her thong. She'd never been so wet before. So *hot*.

Trace let go of the guilt, let go of everything but the fantasy of fucking that cowboy. She slid her fingers into her panties, into her drenched folds, and gasped when she stroked her clit. She was so close to coming, when it usually took her a while to reach orgasm.

With her free hand she cupped one breast and raised it up while lowering her mouth. Her breasts were big enough that she could flick her tongue against her nipple while she fingered her clit.

She closed her eyes, imagining it was Jess who licked her nipples. Jess rubbing his cock against her clit before sliding into her pussy. And how it would feel to have Jess driving into her. She could still feel that long hard length of his cock as he'd pressed up against her on the dance floor. Oh, God. He'd fuck her deep and hard, rough and wild, and he'd make her scream.

A small cry tore from Trace as her orgasm spiked through her, and her eyes flew open. Her hips rocked against her hand as she drew out her orgasm as long as she possibly could, enjoying every electrifying jolt.

When she finished, she collapsed against the seatback, the Mustang suddenly feeling cold as the perspiration on her skin chilled.

Trace leaned forward and banged her forehead against the steering wheel. And then again.

Damn, damn, damn.

She'd just given herself the most amazing orgasm of her life…while fantasizing about another man.

* * * * *

After Jess interrogated Nicole about Trace MacLeod, he tracked down Rick McAllister and found the Border Patrol agent in the sunroom on the main floor. The room smelled like a mixture of Christmas and chlorine from the hot tub under the sun roof and the decorated tree where McAllister was standing. He was in the process of punching off his cell phone and stuffing it into his back pocket.

"Need a favor," Jess said, getting straight to the point as his boots thumped across the hardwood floor to where McAllister stood.

The man gave a quick nod. "Name it and I'll see what I can do."

"Your date, Kathy Newman." Jess jerked his thumb over his shoulder. "Had a few words with Nicole."

The corner of McAllister's mouth quirked. "If I know Nic, I'd say she probably came out on top of any cat fight."

Jess grinned. "Would've laid into the b—, er, woman, if not for a little restraining on my part."

Raising an eyebrow, McAllister said, "I take it Kathy's gone."

"Just left the party."

"Good thing we came in separate vehicles." Rick sighed and shook his head. "What's this favor?"

"I need to find out what Newman knows about Ryan Forrester." With a wry smile, Jess added, "After this incident, it's not likely I'll get anything out of her."

"I'd intended to question her on the bastard, myself." The Border Patrol agent folded his arms across his chest. "Which was why I agreed when she asked me to be her date tonight. With all the evidence we have that Forrester and the drug smugglers are getting the cocaine across the line using UDAs as mules," Rick said, referring to undocumented aliens, or illegal immigrants, "I figured Kathy might know something. Hell, her family owns half the borderland in these parts. Figured I'd see if she might drop a hint, on purpose or by accident."

Hooking his thumbs in his Wranglers, Jess rocked back on his heels. "Not sure that's a woman to bed for info."

"Ah...no." Rick raked his fingers through his dark hair and grimaced. "Let's just say I'm not interested in going where most men in the county have gone before."

Jess snorted back a laugh. "Catch you later in the week and see what you've managed to pry out of Big Tits."

* * * * *

The knot in Trace's belly grew tighter as she drove closer to the Flying M Ranch. She'd changed out of the wild made-for-Nicole-and-not-Trace outfit, and into a pair of worn Levi's, a royal blue scoop-necked t-shirt, thick socks, and Nikes. She'd even taken a moment to tone down the blush on her cheeks with a tissue. Didn't have to worry about the lipstick—Jess had eaten that off.

Shivers skated along Trace's skin at the mere thought. Cripes—when would she be able to push that kiss and that man to the back of her mind?

She guided the Mustang onto the dirt road leading to the MacLeod Ranch. It'd been over four years since she'd been home. Four years since she'd stormed out and told Dee she didn't care if she ever saw her again.

It had taken Trace a long time to realize that Dee had done the best job she could in raising Trace. Sure, there were only a couple of years between the two of them, but Dee had been there for everything when their mother died and their father drew away from them.

In Trace's immaturity, she had seen only that Dee had what Trace didn't—beauty, talent, intelligence… But one day, long after she'd established herself with Wildgames in Europe, it had hit Trace that she did have all that Dee did, she had just needed to recognize her own self-worth. Dee had tried to tell her that time after time, but Trace had let envy—*jealousy*—cloud their relationship.

Eventually, when Trace had moved to England, she'd sent Dee a letter, chatty and friendly, trying to reestablish their relationship. Dee had been warm and receptive, just like she'd always been.

That had been a couple of years ago, and now, Trace had come home. To make amends. To say the things she should have said long ago.

And to finally bury the old, insecure part of herself she should have laid to rest with her troubled childhood.

Countless memories unraveled in Trace's mind as the Mustang's wheels rattled over the cattle guard. She slowed the car down as she drove toward the house.

Toward her *home.*

She'd spent her entire life at the Flying M, up until her two years at the university and then the last four years in Europe. She'd practiced calf-roping and barrel racing in those corrals to the northeast of the ranch house. Despite darkness shrouding the ranch she could easily make out the split rail fencing and the water trough made from a fifty-gallon steel drum.

And over there, in that huge old barn, was where they kept Dancer, Trace's mare. Farther out back she could even see the bunkhouse where most of the ranch hands lived, and she smiled. When she was growing up on the ranch, she'd certainly had her fair share of crushes on hot cowboys.

At the thought of cowboys, one particularly tall and good-looking one came immediately to mind. Amazing—she'd finally been able to forget Jess Lawless for all of what, three minutes?

As she brought the Mustang to a halt in front of the house and switched off the ignition, the knot in her belly rose into her chest, making even breathing difficult. Why was she so anxious about getting together with her sister after all this time? Maybe it was the combination of seeing Dee, and what had happened earlier with Jess.

After she took a couple of deep breaths, Trace climbed out of the car and slammed the door behind her. A dog barked from inside the house and the tawny glow of lights spilled through the kitchen's curtains. She paused for a moment to look up at the now almost clear star-spattered sky. Wow. She'd missed the sight of all those stars. It was so dark out here in the middle of nowhere that stars were far more plentiful and brilliant, and the Milky Way was like white cotton candy spun across the universe.

Dirt and rocks crunched under her shoes as she made herself walk toward the house. Rain-fresh desert air filled her senses, along with the familiar ranch smells of cattle and horses. The weeping willows and oaks had sure grown in the past four years.

Wooden stairs squeaked as she jogged up them to the plant-crowded porch, thick enough that it looked like a small jungle.

A porch light flicked on as Trace reached the front door, and she blinked away the sudden brightness. The rattle of the doorknob caused the knots in her belly and chest to double. Then triple.

The door swung open, but Trace couldn't make out the shadowed figure in the entrance, until the person stepped onto the porch.

Dee. She hadn't changed much in four years — if anything she was more beautiful than ever. Her auburn hair flowed around her shoulders, her skin as flawless and perfect as it had always been.

Only she seemed *happy*. Happier than Trace remembered ever seeing her.

"Yes?" Dee cocked her head, a puzzled smile on her pretty face. "Can I—" Her jaw dropped and her eyes widened. "Trace?"

Trace gave her sister a little smile. "Hey, Dee."

"You brat!" In the next moment Dee had her arms wrapped around Trace, hugging her so tight that the air whooshed out of her lungs. Dee still smelled of orange blossoms, and her embrace was warm and loving. "I missed you so much, knothead," Dee whispered, her voice choked with emotion.

Trace pulled away and smiled, swallowing hard and fighting back tears that she'd never expected. "I missed you, too, string bean. I didn't realize just how much 'til now."

"You look so — so *different*." Dee shook her head as she held Trace by the shoulders and looked her up and down.

"I thought you had to be someone who'd gotten lost or something. Until I saw your eyes. You have Mom's eyes, you know."

A dog barked as though in agreement, and Trace reached down to pet the black and white Border collie. "That's Blue," Dee said as Trace rubbed the dog behind his ears.

"What a gorgeous boy you are," Trace crooned.

"Think you might like to let her in out of the cold?" a masculine voice asked.

Trace's gaze shot up to see Jake Reynolds standing just behind Dee. "*Jake?*" was all Trace could manage as she stood straight and looked at the man who had once been her sister's boyfriend—about ten years ago.

"I was saving this as a surprise." Dee grinned up at Jake before looking back to Trace. "Come on in and say hello to my husband."

"Your *husband?*" Trace stumbled across the threshold as she followed Dee, Jake, and Blue into the ranch house, and let the door swing shut behind her. "You're *married?*"

"Almost two months." Dee held up her left hand, the marquis stone of her wedding band glittering in the light. To each side of the diamond, a peridot was set in the gold band.

"Wow." Trace sighed with admiration. "It's gorgeous."

"Welcome home." Jake settled his arm around Trace's shoulders and gave her a quick squeeze. "Why don't I leave you ladies to catch up while I head to the study?" he said as he released her.

"To watch the end of the football game no doubt." Dee grabbed him by his shirt collar and reached up to brush her lips over his.

"Watch it, woman." Jake's voice rumbled as he wrapped his arms around Dee's waist. "I might just throw you over my shoulder and cart you off to the bedroom, reunion with your sister be damned."

"Mmmm," Dee murmured against his lips. "Promises."

Jake gave Dee a smoldering look that reminded Trace of the way Jess had looked at her earlier. Hot, sensual, and possessive. The kind of look that curled a woman's toes.

He gave Dee a hard kiss and then winked at Trace before walking past the enormous Christmas tree and striding down the hall toward the study.

For a moment Trace had to stand and absorb the living room of the place that had been her home since her birth until she left for Europe. There had been some changes in the past four years. Lots more house plants filled the room that was decorated in a southwestern motif. Navajo rugs were scattered across the tile floor and the walls were covered with a combination of southwestern oil paintings and family portraits. Dee still had all the pictures of Trace and other members of the family on the end tables, as well as lots of new ones that she'd have to spend time looking at later.

The room smelled of pine from the Christmas tree, and of leather from the overstuffed chairs and couches. And there was that old rocker that their mom used to rock them in when they were little, before she'd died.

When Trace's eyes met Dee's, her sister flashed a grin and motioned toward the kitchen. "Let's fill one another in over our favorite chatty food."

"Rocky Road?" Trace laughed as her sister headed toward the freezer with Blue at their heels. "Remember all the times we'd sit at the table with a half gallon of the stuff and eat it straight from the carton with a spoon?"

"Ohhhh, do I ever." Dee laughed and yanked open the freezer door, then dug out the ice cream carton.

After grabbing a couple of clean spoons out of the dishwasher, Dee and Trace settled at the table in the breakfast nook, while Blue curled up at Dee's feet. A peridot heart pendant sparkled at her throat, and Trace shook her head, remembering all those years ago when Dee had said she'd never wear it again.

Incredible how things change. How people change.

The carton made a sucking sound as Trace popped off the lid. "You bought this just because I was coming home, I'll bet."

Dee stuck her spoon into the container and scooped out a spoonful. "Uh-huh." Her gaze lighted on Trace's left ear, and then she tilted her head and looked at Trace's right. "Very cool. Definitely suits your sexy new image."

Trace shook her head and laughed. Thinking of herself as sexy was taking some getting used to.

The sisters spent the next three hours bringing one another up to date on their lives. Dee told Trace how Jake had come back, determined to make up for lost time. "And have we *ever*," she said with a laugh.

Trace shared with Dee all she'd done while living abroad, the places she'd been, the people she worked with, and even a little bit about Harold, the man she'd been dating for the past two years. Yet she couldn't bring herself to tell Dee that she thought he was going to give her an engagement ring for Christmas.

And she definitely couldn't bring up the cowboy she'd met tonight. No, that was better left unsaid.

One kiss, one night, end of story.

But even after the sisters had hugged and said goodnight, and Trace had crawled into the four poster bed in her old bedroom, she couldn't get Jess Lawless off her mind.

Instead she stared up at the canopy looking at the patterns of colorful light on the white fabric that were reflected there from her tiffany lamp with the stained-glass shade. In place of the colors, she saw Jess, reliving every touch of his hands, his lips, his body.

Trace pulled down her nightgown to free her breasts and slipped her fingers into her pussy. As she licked and sucked her own nipples, she imagined that he was watching her masturbate. Would he take his cock in hand and stroke himself as he watched her? Would it turn him on to see her fingering her own pussy and licking her nipples?

Again she imagined that he was sliding his cock into her, filling her. It took only a few strokes of her fingers and she came. Another body wracking orgasm that she had to bite her lip to keep from crying out loud.

She rolled over and switched off the tiffany lamp and relaxed on her pillow.

Only a kiss, she told herself as she finally drifted off to sleep. *It was only a kiss.*

Chapter Four

After the party, Jess headed back to the Flying M Ranch and to the foreman's cabin behind the bunkhouse. Out of habit ingrained from years of training, he made sure the building was secure before he let himself into the small cabin. He'd installed his own security locks on the front and back doors, as well as pull-down shades at the windows, and he always chose a different means of identifying if anyone had been in his quarters in his absence. Today the almost invisible threads had still been intact at both the front and rear entrances, and he found nothing suspicious.

Once he'd made a quick round of the living room, single bedroom, bathroom and kitchen, he slung his duster on the coat rack beside the door. He tossed his Stetson on the knobby top, where it rocked back and forth for a moment before going still.

From out of his duster pocket he withdrew his PDA— a slim palm device. From the holster he pulled out his cell phone and switched it so that it would "hum" instead of vibrate, and then kicked back in the comfortable leather recliner in the cabin's small living room. The room always smelled of mesquite wood from the pile stacked next to the old wood stove and of leather from the worn couch and armchairs.

The furnishings weren't much to look at, but it was neat and clean. A pair of ancient deer antlers was mounted on the wall beside the black stove pipe of the old wood stove. A few throw rugs were scattered around the tiled floor and knotty pine paneled the walls adding to its rustic look.

On one of the small wooden tables perched a small potted Christmas tree with miniature decorations, courtesy of Dee who figured all her ranch hands needed something Christmas-y in their quarters. The tree she'd put in the bunkhouse had been a little too big for his tastes, but the men had gotten a kick out of it.

Jess turned on his palm device and used the stylus to tab through the pages of notes he'd made on the smuggling case and came to his short list of subjects.

Dee MacLeod had been one of his original suspects, but after his first two months of investigations, he'd marked her right off the list.

Kev Grand always seemed to be in the middle of things. He was becoming somewhat of a vigilante as far as UDAs crossing his property. That could be a front. And those poisoned cattle could be just another way to throw suspicion away from his own illegal activities.

Then there was Brad Taylor, who'd been seen around the Wilds' cabin sometime before all the documents had been discovered that had falsely incriminated Steve Wilds. Taylor had claimed to know nothing about it, but he had a habit of staying out late just about every night. Although he'd heard that Taylor had a penchant for twins…at the same time.

According to information Jess had dug up recently, Kathy Newman had a long history with Forrester—too long to be discounted. Apparently they'd been tight for some time, although they'd had some kind of quarrel a few months ago and hadn't been seen together for awhile before the rustling cover had been blown. Big Tits drove a black Mercedes, and the way she was reported to enjoy flashing cash around, it was a wonder Jess hadn't run into her the few months he'd worked the area. Although she did live a good thirty minutes from the MacLeod Ranch, and he'd heard she preferred to spend her money in Sierra Vista, the biggest town in the county, or better yet, Tucson.

Bull Stevens was a big time rancher in the area who also had a big time grudge against UDAs for damaging his fence line. He'd lost thousands of dollars worth of cattle when they strayed out and died after getting into some bad feed. But was that enough to cause a man to get involved with the Mexican drug cartel?

Not too long ago, Natalie Garcia had bought the old Karchner place a couple miles north of the Flying M. Drug activity had escalated since her arrival and some big busts had been made not to far from her property. His gut instinct told him that the single mother had nothing to do with what was going on, but it wouldn't hurt to question her. She was romantically involved with Steve Wilds, who'd been framed but then cleared of any involvement in the rustling activities.

Tomorrow Jess had plans to head down to the county hospital to interview a UDA who'd been used as a mule to smuggle drugs in from Mexico. The man had been beaten half to death by the *coyotes*, the bastards who ran the smuggling operations.

The hum of his cell phone snapped Jess out of his consideration of the suspects to date. He picked up the phone from the end table and saw by the caller ID that it was Santiago.

"Lawless," Jess said into the phone at the same time he shut off the PDA.

"Just talked with Miguel Cotiño," Santiago said.

"The Special Ops Super over at the Border Patrol?"

"Yeah." A feminine giggle could be heard in the background and Santiago's voice lowered. "Said to not bother heading to the hospital to interrogate that mule. He's dead."

"Shit." Jess ground his teeth and thumbed the PDA onto the end table. "Anything else?"

"Nah. Catch you tomorrow. I got me a hot little thing waiting for me to get back to her."

"Later," Jess said before punching the phone off and setting it back down.

At least Santiago was getting some tonight. With a frustrated sigh, Jess got up from the recliner and laid the palm device on the end table. So much for that lead. But what really pissed him off was the fact that those bastard *coyotes* had caused the death of yet another innocent.

Scrubbing his hand over his stubbled face, he considered what to do next. He'd never get to sleep feeling as restless and edgy as he was.

Due to one sexy little redhead who he couldn't get off his mind.

It took only a few minutes to lock up the little cabin and then Jess found himself striding through the dark night and toward the MacLeod house without any real purpose or plan. Just on the hope of seeing Trace, maybe catching her outside or in the kitchen, and getting to talk to her for a few minutes.

He passed by the corrals and barn, the sounds of a horse whickering, the low of a cow and the singsong of crickets filling the night. Jess knew the sounds well. After all, he was a native Texan, and he owned his own nice spread near Houston. Once this case was closed and cleaned up, he intended to head back there. Although he enjoyed his work, he was accustomed to family dropping in, big get-togethers with his folks, his grandma, his sisters and brothers, and all his nieces and nephews. It had been months since he'd seen them, and he could sure use some of his mom's blueberry pie, straight from the oven, with a scoop of homemade vanilla ice cream right on top.

He might even talk to his mom about Trace, about his sudden feeling that she belonged close to the sprawling Lawless family.

Before he knew it, Jess found himself standing in front of the ranch house and near the room he knew had belonged to Trace MacLeod when she was growing up here. No doubt it would be where she'd be sleeping.

What are you going to do, Lawless? Throw rocks at her window?

He bit back a wave of frustration and embarrassment. But then, why the hell not? Maybe she'd get a kick out of it, of him showing her his teenage-feeling interest.

Just around the corner at the back of the house, hidden within a closed in yard, he could hear the pulsing of the hot tub jets as well as Jake's and Dee's voices. By the sound of Dee's gasps and Jake's groans, Jess suspected they were more than enjoying themselves. Better move on from that. Private things were private — though to hear Catie Wilds Savage talk, she wouldn't have thought twice about it. That little hellcat would have pulled up a front row seat and wouldn't be the least embarrassed to admit it.

Jess had never been much for voyeurism, except for once in his teen years, when a kid could be forgiven for being desperate. With a wry smile, he bent and picked up a few pebbles from the yard. Then, he eased behind the trees that obscured the room's window from sight and looked in. Covert operations was something he'd done often, although nothing like this…spying on a woman he was dying to get his hands on, with the intent of grabbing her attention with a pebble or two.

I'm losing my damned mind. And I don't spy on women I'm interested in.

All right, except for that time when he was thirteen and he had peeked into Maggie Jensen's window while she was dressing. She'd been eighteen and built like a brick house — one of those figures that gave all teenage boys wet dreams. It'd been the first time he'd seen a live pair of breasts and a woman's hair-covered mound, and he'd masturbated more than a time or two over the image of her naked, imagining what it would feel like to fuck her.

But now he was an adult, with a raging hard-on for a woman that he couldn't get his mind off.

A few tosses. If she doesn't answer, I'll go on back home.

He melted into the shadows behind the tree as he peered through the parted curtains. Good. The window was closed. He raised his hand for the first pebble toss just about the time he saw Trace lying on her back, staring up at the canopy of the bed. The light beside her bed was on, its stained-glass shade casting rainbow fragments across her face and the pale blue nightgown she wore.

Jess hesitated, hand at the ready, the pebble feeling warm and solid between his fingers.

That gown had thin little straps that would easily break if he tugged on them, and he was sure the silky-looking material would feel soft beneath his hands, just like her skin. The nightgown was hiked up to the top of her thighs, but not quite high enough for him to see anything more than her shapely legs.

Her thighs were squeezed together tightly, and she squirmed a little, as though trying to alleviate an ache there. But in the next moment she reached her hands up and pulled at the top of her nightgown, freeing both her breasts.

Jess dropped his arm back to his side. The pebble — hell, all the pebbles — fell out of his hands.

The woman had damn perfect breasts with cherry dark nipples just begging for his mouth.

His cock bucked against the denim of his jeans. He knew he should have some moral battle inside, but the reaction was too strong, too deep. This woman, oh, yeah, she was his. He had claimed her at Nicole's, and he was claiming her again, right there under her sister's tree.

He unbuckled his belt, unzipped his jeans, and released his aching cock. With slow familiar strokes he moved his hand up and down the length of his cock as he watched Trace cup her breasts and squeeze her nipples.

"Yeah, that's it, sugar," he murmured as she slipped one hand down and then she spread her legs wide as though welcoming him between her thighs.

She hitched her nightgown up around her waist and his groin tightened when he saw she wasn't wearing any underwear. "That's one beautiful pussy," he said softly as he worked his cock. "Can't wait to fuck you."

Trace's fingers slipped between her folds and she began rubbing her clit in a slow, circular motion. With her free hand she pushed up one of her generous breasts and flicked her tongue against her own nipple.

Damn but that turned him on. He'd never watched a woman licking and sucking her own nipples, and the sight was damn arousing.

Her fingers grew more frantic and his strokes more intense.

When she came, she threw back her head, and she bit her lip as though to keep from crying out. Her body trembled and vibrated, and she kept rubbing her clit until she came a second time.

As her body relaxed, a dreamy expression covered her face, and he only hoped she'd been imaging that he was fucking her. She raised her fingers to her nose as though to smell her juices, and that was enough to make Jess's climax hit him in a rush.

He bit the inside of his cheek as his come squirted onto the plants outside Trace's bedroom window. Damn that had felt good. But the real thing was going to feel a whole lot better once she was ready to take his cock inside her pussy.

Trace rolled over and switched off the light, plunging her room into darkness. Jess fixed his belt and jeans, and melted out into the night.

* * * * *

Trace waved her sister and new brother-in-law off as Jake's black truck sped down the dusty road. They had a holiday party to attend in Tucson, and had decided to spend the night at a resort there, rather than making the hundred-plus mile drive back the same night. Dee had wanted Trace to come, but Trace had begged off, telling her sister that she still needed to recover from jetlag. Besides, she had to let Harold know she'd arrived safely, and she wanted to e-mail Lani and a couple of her other friends, too.

For a moment she stayed on the porch, enjoying what was left of the early evening sunshine. The December desert air smelled so fresh and clean. Over the Mule Mountains to the west, the sun hung low, teasing the sky with wisps of lavender, peach, and mauve. Blue, Dee's Border Collie, raised his head and sniffed the wind, then trotted off toward the barn.

Trace turned her gaze to the east, to the tawny mountains rising behind the ranch. She'd explored those mountains many times with her sister when they were younger. Memories of the fun times they'd shared returned clear and crisp, like they'd happened last week instead of years ago.

A glint caught her eye, coming from the mountain. About where that little hideaway of Dee's and Jake's used to be—several quick flashes. Like a mirror reflecting the sunlight. Probably some campers, or hikers. Maybe even some illegals, sneaking to greener pastures.

Trace ran her palms up and down her upper arms, rubbing away the evening chill as she turned on her heel and headed back into the house. After she shut the door tight behind her, the complete quiet of the house settled over Trace, reminding her of times she'd been home alone as a teenager, and Dee had been off working the ranch. Would she ever get over the guilt of having left all the ranch's responsibilities to Dee?

Pausing in mid-step, Trace's gaze drifted over family photographs displayed prominently around the room. Pictures of her with Dee, of each of them alone, and with their parents. After their father took off with his new wife and left them alone, Trace had refused to contact him. He never took the time to see how she was doing, so why should she bother?

Trace moved to one of the end tables, stopped in front of her senior photo, and slid her fingers along the wooden frame. In the picture her face was pudgy, her smile soft and wistful. Despite the wire framed glasses she used to wear, her green eyes were bright and full of hope for the future.

Next to her senior photo was a recent picture of Dee and Jake. She was standing in his embrace, her face tilted up to his, and the way he was looking at her with so much love, it made Trace's heart ache with both pleasure for her sister, and envy for herself.

She still couldn't believe Dee was married to Jake, after all these years. Trace had to admit they made the perfect couple now, as they had a decade ago. There was so much fire and passion between the two of them then, and now…*wow*. To have sparks like that. Trace hadn't thought that kind of passion between a man and a woman could possibly be real—just something she'd read about in romance novels.

That was, until she'd met Jess.

With a groan of frustration, Trace jerked herself away from the photographs, skirted the Christmas tree and started down the hall. Why the hell did that cowboy keep popping into her mind? Maybe what she needed was a nice, long, relaxing bath.

Better yet, a dip in the hot tub would be perfect. They'd always kept it heated and had used it year round. Knowing Dee, it still would be ready for use.

In her bedroom, Trace kicked off her Nikes and yanked off her socks, then ditched her jeans and t-shirt.

After she'd donned a short terry robe over her bra and underwear, she grabbed a thick towel and headed out to the hot tub in the enclosed backyard.

The French doors squeaked as she opened them, and then again as she closed the doors behind her. There was a definite coolness to the air by Arizona standards, and the steam rising off the top of the water in the sunken tub was a welcome sign. Thank goodness Dee had the outdoor heaters set up close to the hot tub to take the chill out of the air. The pole heaters were easily six feet tall with tops that looked like woks turned upside down.

Trace tossed her towel onto a deck chair and flipped on the heaters. In moments their elements began to glow rich orange-red, the same color as the sun sinking in the west. After she turned on the whirlpool jets, Trace dropped her robe onto a lounge chair. For a moment she stood on the redwood decking in only her royal blue satin bra and panties. With one little adjustment of her hairclip, she piled her hair up on top of her head so that it would stay out of the water.

The whirlpool bubbled and frothed like a witch's cauldron—even the lights beneath the surface appeared green and eerie, as though it truly was a magical potion. She started forward then hesitated.

What the hell. She was alone—the backyard was completely enclosed. It was secluded and hidden from view by countless trees and bushes, so no one could see her. And Dee and Jake would be gone 'til tomorrow.

Trace stripped out of her bra and bikini underwear, her nipples growing painfully hard in the cool air. When she walked in front of one heater, its warmth radiated along one side, the chilly air brushing her other side.

She stepped down into the hot tub and sighed in complete bliss as she sank into the warmth and settled onto the underwater bench. Jets of water pulsated along her skin while she breathed deep of the clear and clean country evening air. She'd forgotten how dry the Arizona desert was—it felt somehow lighter here than in England.

While she relaxed, for the millionth time her thoughts returned to last night.

To Jess Lawless.

Everything about the man screamed sex. Rough, wild, and hard...all that Harold couldn't begin to give her.

No, Harold couldn't be considered wild about anything...anything other than Wildgames, that was. He was a shrewd businessman, but he was calm and refined as a boyfriend and as a lover. There'd never been any fireworks with him, but it had always been comfortable and enjoyable.

Trace rolled her gaze heavenward and stared into the darkening sky and sighed. Here she was, thinking about her possible future husband, and she could muster up no real enthusiasm for their sexual relationship.

But when she thought of that cowboy...there was nothing remotely calm or unemotional about how he'd made her feel. In just that short time she'd been with him, he'd made her feel sexy and *alive.*

Infatuation, Trace, that's all it is. The grass is always greener...

She closed her eyes and focused on the feel of the heaters warming the back of her head, the water bubbling at her nipples and jets pulsating along her legs. Spreading her thighs, she adjusted her hips so that one of the jets aimed right at her pussy. *Mmmm, yeah.* That felt so good.

She could almost imagine Jess licking her right where the water pulsed. Maybe he'd bite her there...not too hard, but enough that it would drive her even crazier for want and need of him.

Trace slipped the fingers of one hand between her thighs and into her slit. Even through the water she could feel the creaminess of her desire, the slickness of her pussy.

She brought her other hand to her breast and kneaded and plucked her nipple. Eyes still closed, she fantasized about sucking her own nipples while Jess devoured her pussy. She raised her breast and flicked her tongue across the hard nub. A pleasant warm lick that immediately chilled in the night air until she licked it again.

Her fingers aided the jets, stroking her clit harder and harder, her tongue flicking again and again over her nipple, urging her closer and closer to climax. Imagining Jess's tongue all over her body. Imagining Jess sliding his cock into her core—

The squeak of the French doors jolted Trace from her fantasy.

Her eyes snapped open and she jerked her head up to see the large figure of a man. He stood beside the hot tub, his face shadowed by a dark cowboy hat.

"Welcome home, Trace MacLeod," he murmured.

Chapter Five

Jess.

Trace would recognize that deep, sensual drawl anywhere.

Omigod.

Heated embarrassment prickled her skin. She wanted to die from humiliation at being caught masturbating—by the very man she'd been fantasizing about. And darn it if her brain and mouth hadn't taken another vacation. She slid further beneath the water so that her breasts were hidden by the bubbles and crossed her arms over her chest for good measure.

"Uh-uh." He crouched down beside the hot tub, and pushed his Stetson up with one finger. She could clearly see his roguish blue eyes in the waning evening light. "Keep going, sugar."

"What—" Trace swallowed, her throat incredibly dry. "Ah, what are you doing here, Jess? How did you find me?"

"Later." He reached out his hand and ran his thumb along her lower lip, causing more warmth to spread throughout her—but this time it was from arousal. "Right now you're gonna make yourself come."

Trace sucked in her breath. "You want me to...in front of you?"

"Oh, yeah." His sensual smile and the way he was touching her almost made her climax on the spot. "I want you to finger yourself while I watch. But first you're going to move up a little higher to give me a better view."

Face burning, she shook her head, pulling away from his touch. "I—I can't, um, do it in front of you."

"You can." Jess caught her chin in his hand and forced her to look at him. "And you will."

Trace trembled, yet managed to ask, "And if I don't?"

His eyes glittered with dark sensuality. "I'll pull you out of that hot tub, lay you across my knee and spank your sexy ass."

Oh. My. God.

At the visualization of him doing just that, Trace's eyes widened, her pussy aching with a wild urgency. The need to have Jess inside her, and to have him *now*, exploded through her like a storm.

But she couldn't have sex with this man, this cowboy—although for the life of her, she wasn't able to remember why not.

His fingers slid in a slow and sensuous movement from her chin, along her jaw line. "Now what'll it be?"

She was almost tempted to let him spank her—the thought was strangely erotic.

Trembling with nervousness and desire, Trace eased up until she was sitting on the redwood decking, her feet still in the frothing waters of the hot tub. Her nipples chilled as hard as gold nuggets, and goose bumps roughened her flesh. She quickly warmed from the heaters at her back, but it was mostly Jess's touch that set her on fire as his fingertips skated from her lips and down her neck to the hollow of her throat where he lightly caressed the soft skin.

The night smelled of desert air and of Jess's masculine scent and his spicy aftershave, and her senses whirled. Her blood thrummed even harder in her veins, the sound loud enough to nearly drown out the pulsing of the hot tub.

She held her breath as he moved his hand along her collarbone, and over the gentle rise of her breast. "Spread your legs," he said in that drawl that made her clit throb.

Trace widened her thighs, her feet dangling in the churning waters, while keeping her gaze focused on Jess. It was as if she had no choice but to do as he commanded. No will of her own. Or was it that his will *was* the same as hers...what she really wanted.

"Sweet." Jess settled on one knee as he cupped her breast with his large hand, his powerful t-shirt-clad chest brushing against her arm. "Touch your clit."

Shivers raced through her as she braced herself with one palm behind her on the decking, and slipped the fingers of her other hand through the soft curls of her mound and into the slick heat of her wet folds.

"Yeah, that's it." His voice rumbled as he caressed her nipple with his thumb.

She trembled, so close to coming. Just a little more—

"Stop." At his command her fingers came to a halt and she wanted to scream. "You're not gonna come just yet." He moved his hand to her other breast. "Slide two fingers into your pussy and hold them there."

Oh, God, this man was going to kill her.

Trace's whole body vibrated as she obeyed and pressed her knuckles against her folds. The feelings were so intense it was as if Jess's fingers were inside her.

With his free hand, he took off his Stetson and tossed it onto a deck chair. "Thrust out your chest so that I can get a real good look at your breasts."

Two fingers still deep inside herself, Trace arched her back. Her nipples had hardened to such sensitive nubs that the lightest brush of his fingers sent lightning bolts of sensation through her. "Jess, I can't take anymore."

"We've just gotten started." His hand moved away from her breasts and he stood in a quick, fluid movement. She lifted her chin to watch him as he jerked his t-shirt over his head and tossed it onto the deck chair beside his hat.

Dang, but that man had a fine chest. Chiseled muscles that made her want to run her fingers over every sculpted contour down to his flat hard six-pack abs. Thick veins ran along his bulging biceps to his large hands, hands that she wanted all over her. She'd never seen a man so up close and personal with such a fine body.

His hands moved to his western buckle, and in no time he'd unfastened it and set the belt aside, then toed off his boots and peeled off his socks.

Oh jeez. Oh cripes. He was going to get completely naked.

Hurry, darn it.

As if he'd heard her thoughts, Jess smiled and unfastened his jeans and slid them down over his hips. His thick, luscious cock sprang out at full attention as he pushed his jeans past his heavily muscled thighs.

Wow, wow, wow. His cock was even bigger than she'd thought when she'd felt it pressed against her at the Christmas party. It curved up a bit, rather than just being straight. Dang but that would feel good…

A sense of lightheadedness swept over Trace and she realized she was holding her breath. She gulped in the fresh evening air, her heart beating faster and faster as Jess slid out of his jeans and briefs. She watched the ripple and play of his muscles while he strode toward her and stepped into the hot tub.

When he was waist-deep in the water, he moved between her thighs, pressing her knees apart, and braced his hands on the decking at either side of her hips. He pushed his cock against her hand, forcing her own fingers deeper into her pussy.

Oh, God. She couldn't. She could. She wanted. She shouldn't…

"We don't have protection," she finally whispered.

"I can satisfy you in more ways than you can imagine." He leaned forward and nuzzled her ear, and then ran his hot tongue along the row of earrings. "Now…," he murmured, "back to where we left off."

That's all the man had to do—talk in that deep, sensual drawl, and she'd do just about anything for him.

Anything at all.

"Stroke your clit." He lowered his head and nuzzled her breast, his warm breath fanning across her nipple as he spoke. "Nice 'n slow."

She slid her fingers out of her core, slick with her juices, and stroked her tight nub. Jess flicked his tongue over her nipple and Trace arched her back toward him, needing him to take her deeper into his mouth.

But he moved to her other nipple and scraped his stubble over the sensitive flesh. "While you're fingering yourself," he murmured, "imagine that I'm sliding my cock into your pussy."

Trace's breathing came quick and uneven. As her finger rubbed faster at her clit, her eyelids drifted shut. *God*. She was a trigger away from climaxing.

"Look at me," he demanded and her eyes popped open. He smiled, and with one hand he caught the back of her head and brought her toward him. With a flick of his wrist, he pulled out her hair clip, allowing her hair to tumble down around her shoulders and to slide below her shoulder blades like a sensual caress.

The clip clattered on the decking as Jess cupped the back of her head. Her fingers continued to stroke her clit as he brought his mouth above hers. She tasted his warm breath upon her lips, bringing back a rush of memories of that incredible first kiss from last night.

"When I fuck you, sugar," he said, his gaze locked with hers, "you're gonna watch my cock slide into you. You'll watch me possess you. I'll fuck you so deep you'll feel it in your throat."

His words magnified Trace's arousal. She gasped and started to cry out as her orgasm began to ripple through her. But Jess brought his mouth down hard and kissed her with such savage intensity that her orgasm multiplied. Her hips rocked against her hand, his cock rubbing against her knuckle as he pressed himself against her. Trace's world and thoughts spun as he devoured her in a kiss she never wanted to end.

When she finally stopped convulsing, he broke away. Trace could only stare at him, tasting him on her tongue, her face burning from the scrape of his stubble, her fingers still lodged between her thighs.

He took her hand, slipping her fingers into her folds and then out, and brought it to his face. He breathed deep, and a pained expression crossed his rugged features. "I've got to sample you," he said and then slid her fingers into his mouth, licking her juices from them with sensual swirls of his tongue.

Oh my God, was all Trace could think. *Oh, my God.*

Jess's cock strained toward Trace, dying to get inside her slick heat. Her unique flavor only made him want her more, and he gritted his teeth to hold himself in check. He wanted to take her right out here in the hot tub and fuck her 'til she couldn't walk for a month of Sundays.

And the way she was looking at him, her jade eyes an even darker green, her skin flushed from her orgasm, and her body trembling with desire…he had no doubt she'd let him in.

If this was any woman but Trace MacLeod, he'd slide into her pussy and claim her now.

But Trace was different. He'd known it from the first time he'd seen her photo in the MacLeod living room. And when he'd met her, even when he hadn't recognized her by her appearance, he'd known this was one special woman.

Jess had no doubt in his mind that he'd have her — he just had to make sure that she'd be ready, and there'd be not a single regret when he made her his.

And *only* his.

But for now, he had to taste her — thoroughly.

Kneeling on the hot tub's underwater bench, he placed his palms on the inside of her pale thighs and pressed.

"Jess." His name was a gasp on her lips as she slid her hands into his hair.

He breathed deep of her scent as he nuzzled the soft curls of her mound. "Damn you smell good," he said, then trailed his tongue down her slit, over the fine hair to the sensitive skin between her pussy and her ass.

She clung to him as he held her thighs tight in his hands and licked the bottom of each of her ass cheeks then gave the soft flesh gentle bites.

He was feeling anything but gentle. It was all he could do to continue his slow seduction. A sexy woman like Trace would enjoy some hard and fast sex, but Jess wanted to give her more than that—and take more, too. In fact, he wanted her heart, because he aimed to keep her.

The thought surprised him, yet at the same time he didn't question it.

Trace's soft moans became louder and more urgent as Jess worked his way back to her drenched folds. Her fingers clenched tighter in his hair as he dipped his tongue into her slit, tasting her full potency.

Her thighs trembled as he flicked his tongue over her clit, and he pulled away. "Not yet," he said against her flesh, and then thrust his tongue into her hot core.

That purring sound rose up from Trace as he licked and sucked at her pussy. Her taste and smell, the feel of her body beneath his hands, all made his cock so hard he could probably bench-press with it. All he'd have to do was rise up and plunge into her heat and fuck her. He could almost imagine how his balls would slap against her ass and how it would feel to be buried inside her.

His rampant thoughts added fuel to the intensity of his desire for Trace. He plunged two fingers inside her, and as she cried out he nipped at her clit.

She screamed. Her body rocked against his mouth, and she gripped his hair like she was busting a bronc. He pressed his face even harder against her pussy, licking and sucking her as she bucked, coming again and yet again.

"I want you to stand with your back to me now," Jess said while she was still trembling with her orgasm.

Trace audibly caught her breath. "I don't know if I can."

"Sure you can, sugar. I've got to see that beautiful ass of yours." He could barely keep his hands off her as she turned and stood on the underwater bench, facing away from him, her ass well out of the water. "That's real nice," he murmured as he cupped her smooth cheeks with his palms. "Brace your hands on the decking."

His hands spread her ass cheeks apart so that he could see her puckered anus, and he could just imagine sliding into that tight rear hole. He slipped his fingers through her slick pussy juices and smoothed them back.

"Oh...my..." Trace's voice wavered as he circled her anus, and then she gasped as he slid the tip of his middle finger inside.

Tight, but not too tight. She'd be a nice fit. "How does that feel?" he said as he slowly pushed his finger all the way to his knuckle.

"Good." She let out a soft moan as he slowly moved his finger in and out of her anus. "Really, really good."

"You've been fucked in the ass before?" he asked, then gritted his teeth at the thought of any other man sharing this with her.

"Never." Trace shook her head, her hair sliding over her back with the movement. "But I—I have fantasized about it."

Jess relaxed. He'd damn sure be the only man who'd do it, too. He increased the motion of his finger, and she rocked her hips back and forth and rode his hand. "You've played with toys...stuck a dildo or two up your ass, haven't you?" he asked, and stopped the motion of his finger but kept it lodged inside her.

"Yes." A whimper escaped Trace's throat. "Don't stop, Jess."

"I'm not through with you yet." Jess slipped his finger out and then in the next instant, he scooped Trace up.

She gasped as she found herself suddenly on her back in his embrace, and she threw her arms around his neck. "What are you doing?"

Instead of answering her question, he eased onto the underwater bench in the hot tub and cradled her in his lap. He fondled one of her nipples with his thumb, and she squirmed on his lap. "Why'd you run out on me last night?"

Trace moaned, so incredibly aroused from what he'd been doing to her just seconds ago. "I—dang. I can't even think when you do that."

Jess gave a soft chuckle. "Try."

"Fear." She swallowed, her eyes heavy-lidded as her arousal grew. "I was afraid if I stayed around you, something would happen. Something like this."

"What's wrong with what we're doing?" he asked softly.

"You know." She could feel heat rise in her cheeks. "This is cheating. That kiss last night was cheating."

"It's not cheating when you're movin' on." He held her tighter with one arm and continued his exploration of her body with his other hand. "He's not right for you."

Her gaze met his as she tried to straighten in his arms. "You've never even met Harold."

Jess grinned. "Harold?"

Trace tilted her head up and glared at him. "He's a great guy. Kind, gentle, thoughtful."

"You're too passionate a woman for kind and gentle." Jess slid his palm down her flat belly toward her mound and felt her tremble beneath his touch. "After awhile you'd feel bored and trapped. Wouldn't be fair to either one of you."

Frowning, she placed her palm on his bare chest, like she was bracing herself. "You don't even know me."

"Better than you think." One hand rested on her belly as he slipped the other into her hair and rubbed the base of her scalp in a slow, sensuous movement. "You're confident in your work, but insecure in yourself. You're sexy and gorgeous, but you don't even realize how beautiful you are." When she dropped her jaw in surprise, he gave her a smile. "The time I first saw your eyes, it was plain as day."

Trace stared at Jess, amazed and unable to speak for a moment. The churning waters of the hot tub filled her ears along with the sound of her own heartbeat. "We just met."

"The pictures Dee keeps in the family room." He gently continued massaging the back of her head as the jets caressed her body. "Months ago when I saw those photos of you, I thought you'd be worth getting to know real well."

Prickles raced along her skin. "Who *are* you?"

"Foreman for the Flying M." He shrugged. "Been here 'bout six months."

"You live and work here?" Trace clenched her fist against his chest, her thoughts spinning. "At the ranch?"

The corner of his mouth quirked and he nodded. "Uh-huh."

Oh, lord.

"That's just great." She rested her head against his muscled chest. "That's like leaving Eve in the garden of Eden. Irresistible temptation within walking distance."

Jess chuckled, his chest vibrating beneath her ear. "Irresistible, huh?"

Shifting on his lap, she felt the hard insistence of his cock pressed against her ass, and could hardly form a coherent thought for a moment. What if he slid into her tight rear hole and fucked her now?

Taking a deep breath, she said, "I don't know what it is, but you make me forget everything." She leaned back and tilted her head to look at him. "Except you. All I can think about is you. And I barely even know you, Jess Lawless."

"That's as good a start as any." He adjusted her in his lap, turning her so that she was straddling him, his cock pressed against the soft curls of her mound. "For now I want to see you come again."

She laced her fingers around his neck and arched her back as he leaned down to flick his tongue over her nipple. The damp ends of her hair rubbed over her back as she moaned and squirmed on his lap, against his erection...dying to feel him inside her, yet hesitating to take that step, to cross that boundary.

Jess slid his forefinger between her thighs as he licked and sucked and gently bit her nipples. Harder he stroked her clit, bringing her closer to yet another orgasm.

"I can hardly wait to be inside you, Trace," he murmured against one nipple. "I want to thrust into your pussy and fuck you now so bad I can taste it."

"Yes," Trace whispered as she rode his fingers. "You're so big. You'll feel so good."

He groaned and bit harder at her nipple, causing Trace to cry out with the pleasure and the pain of his teeth sinking into her soft flesh. His cock pressed against her belly as his hand worked her clit, and she wondered when he was going to slide inside her.

Deep. Hard. Fast.

Just the thought was enough to push her over the edge. A furious climax stole her breath and all her senses, going on and on until she collapsed against his chest.

She expected him to raise her up, to drive his cock into her core.

Instead it sounded as though he was speaking through clenched teeth as he said, "I've got to go before I lose what's left of my control."

"What?" Trace rose up to look at him, but he grasped her waist with his big hands, moved her aside and set her on the bench. "What are you doing?" she asked as he strode out of the hot tub.

He snatched the towel off the deck chair and rubbed it over his body. Even while she was confused by his sudden actions, she couldn't help but admire his muscled body.

Talk about prime choice cowboy ass!

But when he started to yank on his jeans, she scrambled out of the hot tub to stand beside him, water trailing over her body and pooling about her feet.

"You're gonna catch a chill," he muttered, taking the now damp towel and rubbing it over her shoulders. "I intended to grab a fresh towel for you."

Conflicting emotions stormed through her. Was he rejecting her now that he knew she wanted him? Was that why he was leaving? Yet he was rubbing the towel over her so gently, and instinctively she knew this man didn't play games.

"Why are you getting dressed?" she asked as he dried her thighs, the soft hair of her mound, and on down to her calves.

"If I stay around you any longer I'm going to fuck you, sugar," he all but growled.

"Isn't that what we both want?" she whispered.

Only the sound of the bubbling hot tub and a smattering of chirping crickets were her response. Jess stood, grabbed her bathrobe off the deckchair, helped her slip it on, then tied the sash with a rough tug.

"When I make love to you," he finally said, his voice still rough with desire, "no man is gonna come between us." He caught her cheeks in his calloused palms and forced her to look at him. "No doubts. No fears. No regrets. Understand?"

Trace nodded, unable to speak. Barely able to think.

Jess gave her a quick, fierce kiss, then grabbed his boots and t-shirt and strode into the house without looking back.

Chapter Six

Cool December winds brushed Trace's cheeks as she strolled across the yard toward the barn. She loved how mild the winters were here, and surprisingly she liked how dry it was, too. Although she loved it there, England could get a little rainy and dreary at times.

She still couldn't believe what had happened two nights ago at the hot tub. Every time she thought about Jess — naked and doing the things he'd been doing to her — her stomach twisted and her body had an instant reaction. She swore she was walking around with permanently soaked panties and her nipples poking through her t-shirt like someone had stuck jelly beans in her bra.

Out of the corner of her eye she spotted a couple of cowboys at the corrals, but she refused to look outright to see if Jess might be there. Of course she knew she really didn't have to *see* him to know whether or not he was near. If he had been, she'd have been able to sense him, to *feel* his presence.

When she reached the shadowed interior of the barn, Trace paused for a moment to allow her eyes to become accustomed to the dark. The old alarm bell still hung where it always had been, right at the barn's entrance. That thing would wake the dead, her dad had always said. It was painted gold and kind of looked like a church bell, only smaller. And much louder, according to her father.

Scents of alfalfa hay and sweet grain washed over her, along with odors of horse and liniment. Every smell was unique and brought back individual memories from all the years she'd grown up here.

When she'd come into the barn yesterday to practice her kickboxing in the storage room, and to see her old mare Dancer, she'd been surrounded by countless memories from her childhood. She'd worked up a good sweat while kickboxing, practicing her kicks, punches, and jabs, enjoying being back at the ranch. That feeling of being home had wrapped around her like a warm blanket, making her feel relaxed and secure.

But England was home now. She didn't *want* the Flying M to feel like home. She had success and everything that went along with it, including a promising future.

Trace wandered toward the ranch office that was close to the barn entrance and her thoughts turned to Jess. He hadn't been back to the house since the experience in the hot tub, and she'd been both thankful and disappointed. Every time someone came to the front door her heart would start pounding, and she'd expect it to be Jess, but he'd stayed away. Maybe he was too busy, or maybe he was having second thoughts about pursuing her.

Wow. Just the thought of that man pursuing her never failed to give her a little shiver down the small of her back. Somehow she didn't think he was the type to give up when he'd found something he wanted. And *wow*, he wanted *her*.

Yesterday she'd watched him from the back door of the barn, keeping to the shadows, but she'd been close enough to hear his deep voice, to see the powerful flex of his muscles beneath his denim western work shirt. If only she'd been able to see those incredible blue eyes...but they'd been hidden by his black Stetson.

Jess had been instructing a younger ranch hand, helping the teenager train his horse for roundup. She'd been impressed with how patiently Jess had worked with the boy, never acting a bit frustrated when the teenager made some real greenhorn mistakes. Jess had just taken the boy right through each step again.

Trace smiled at the Christmas wreath hanging on the door of the barn office as she let herself in. Dee certainly got into the holiday spirit all over the ranch. The heavy oak door silently closed behind Trace on well-oiled hinges as she headed to the huge desk. That desk had been around since the days of the old west, when her great-great grandpa MacLeod had claimed this stretch of land for the Flying M. The surface of the desk was glossy from years of use and smelled of lemon oil that her sister probably used to keep it in such beautiful condition.

The room was paneled in rich oak, and the leather couch and chair were all in a deep ox blood brown. It was much like it had always been, but she could see Dee's touch in the gingham curtains at the room's only window, and in the small Christmas tree on the table between the couch and overstuffed chair. Family photos were in here, too, and it touched Trace to see that her sister had pictures of all of them close to her when she worked.

To the left of the desk were a couple of huge file cabinets, along with a computer station where Dee kept all the ranch records and did payroll. Best of all, it had internet access.

Before Trace sat down to check her e-mail, she reached for the bottle of hand lotion perched on one corner of the old oak desk. She squirted a generous amount of the thick stuff onto her hands and rubbed it into her dry skin. The lotion smelled like brown sugar and vanilla, a warm, comforting scent.

After she'd wiped the excess off her fingers with a tissue from a box on the desk, Trace perched on the swivel chair in front of the computer workstation. Dee had really brought the ranch a long way into the future. Their dad had never bothered with computers, but after Dee went to college and came home to take over the ranch, she made some big changes—all for the better.

When Trace downloaded her e-mail, she scanned her inbox and bit her lower lip when she came to an e-mail from Harold, sent just hours ago. For a moment she hesitated, almost afraid to open it, as if he'd already know what she'd done with a certain blue-eyed cowboy. No, she hadn't fucked him, but as guilty as she felt, she might as well have.

Funny thing was that up until now she had only felt confused, and not like she'd done something wrong.

Like it had been meant to happen.

Like maybe she and Harold weren't meant to be together after all.

She took a deep breath and opened the e-mail from Harold and could almost hear his refined British accent in his post:

Dearest Tracilynn,

I miss you, love. Haven't received word from you since your arrival in Tucson three days ago. Did you make it safely to your sister's home? If I do not hear from you by ten tonight, I shall call. I look forward to joining you in Arizona at Christmas.

H

Trace stared at the message for a few moments, not really seeing it at all. In place of Harold's aristocratic looks, sandy blond hair, and his warm brown eyes, she saw a dark and dangerous man in a black Stetson…

Shaking her head, like that might work to shake loose the image of Jess, Trace hit the reply button. She wasn't ready to talk to Harold in person, not yet, and wanted to make sure he didn't call. She didn't know what to say, and there was no way she could talk to him until she figured everything out.

If that was even possible.

But she would call him, and soon. She just needed a few more days.

Chicken.

Trace responded with a short e-mail, telling Harold that she'd arrived and was still recovering from jetlag, and that she planned to call him the following weekend.

Pushing thoughts of Harold aside, she ran through the rest of her messages. All work related e-mails she ignored since she was on vacation, and just read the personal notes. She was pleased to see one from Lani Stanton, who sounded positive despite the rough divorce she was going through. If anyone deserved a good man, it was that girl.

When she came to Gail's note, Trace had to laugh out loud. Her next door neighbor in London was a hoot, and she kept trying to get Trace to read erotic romance e-books. Trace hadn't had a chance to visit the romantica site yet, but she'd just have to break down and do it. Especially after what she'd experienced with Jess.

Trace closed her eyes for a moment, trying to block out those images, but it only made them stronger. Her fingers moved to her ear out of habit, and she played with her earrings as she visualized Jess as he had been the night at the hot tub. She could almost smell his spicy aftershave, his unique masculine scent and could almost feel the heat of his body close to hers—

The door slammed shut behind Trace, shattering her fantasy.

Her eyelids popped open and she swiveled on the seat and saw that it was her sister. The disappointment she felt that it wasn't Jess caught her off guard. "No fair sneaking up on me like that," Trace said.

With a mischievous grin, Dee plopped down onto the overstuffed leather couch, and tossed a bundle of mail onto the cushion beside her. "Ran into Catie at the Safeway grocery store in town. We figured a game of cards might be fun this Saturday night. Poker. You up for it?"

"Sure." Trace tried to muster up some enthusiasm. At least it would get her mind off of Jess for a while.

Dee glanced at the computer. "Checking in with your boyfriend?"

With a shrug, Trace said, "Yeah."

Cocking her head to one side, Dee asked, "Something wrong? You don't seem all that enthusiastic."

Trace forced a smile and shook her head. "Just a bit of jetlag."

"Take a nap. Get some rest, kiddo." Dee scooped up the pile of mail and started flipping through the pieces as she spoke. "I didn't expect you to help out with the chores. And here you've already mucked out Imp's and Dancer's stalls, not to mention cleaning out the back storage room."

"Hey, Jake set up that punching bag for me there, so it was the least I could do." Trace smiled. "And besides, it's kinda nice to do those things again."

The corner of Dee's mouth quirked. "Then by all means…" Her voice trailed off and her expression turned puzzled as she held up a postcard. She flipped it over, and then her face paled, her fingers going to her throat in that all too familiar movement that told Trace her sister was upset about something.

"What's the matter?" Trace said, even as she moved from her chair to slide onto the couch beside her sister.

"I'll have to tell Jake." Dee shook her head, her lips pursed. "This is a bunch of bullshit."

Trace reached for the card and Dee let it slip from her fingers. As Trace looked over the note, her sister got up and started pacing the floor.

On one side was an odd design of letters within letters. A capital B in red was a kind of border, and then a Capital I in green was a little smaller in the middle, and then a T in blue a tad smaller than that. And to the left side of the T was a yellow C and to the right was an orange H…

BITCH.

Trace's skin chilled, goose bumps pebbling her skin as she turned the card over.

In a messy black scrawl was written:

It's not over, you double-crossing bitch.

"Shit," Dee muttered, snapping Trace's attention from the card and to her sister, who was still pacing the floor. "I bet it's Forrester."

"Who?" Trace tossed the card onto the couch like it was contaminated. "And why would he send something like this?"

Dee stopped pacing and explained to Trace how the former deputy sheriff had been caught red-handed stealing cattle from Kev Grand. It had turned out that Ryan had masterminded all the rustling that had been going on in the area for months. Dee had lost thousands of dollars in cattle, as had Kev, the Wilds, and a few other neighboring ranches.

"Only problem was, Ryan got away." Dee fingered the peridot heart pendant at her throat. "Jake can't tell me anything, since it relates to a case he's involved with. But Catie Wilds, er Savage, said she heard that Ryan had used the rustling as a cover for something bigger. Since Jake is Customs, for him to be involved it's got to be some kind of contraband, like illegal arms or drugs, or even computers."

"So what's this got to do with anything?" Trace asked.

Dee shook her head. "My gut says Jake and Savage are very close to something, and Forrester's concerned we're going to stumble right over it and him."

* * * * *

Without bringing attention to himself, Jess hitched one hip against the doorframe of the MacLeod kitchen and folded his arms across his chest as he watched Trace and Dee prepare a taco dinner.

It'd been six days since the night at the hot tub, but he could still taste Trace…the flavor of her kiss and the juices between her thighs. Damn but she had a sweet pussy. His cock grew tight against his jeans and he shifted slightly, hoping that Dee wouldn't notice he had a major hard-on once she realized he was there.

Grease popped and crackled on the stovetop as Dee dipped a corn tortilla into the hot liquid to make a taco shell. Warm aromas of seasoned meat, Mexican rice, and refried beans made Jess's stomach growl.

Still neither of the women noticed him, and it gave him a few moments to study Trace as she diced a tomato on a wooden cutting board. Wisps of strawberry blonde hair fell into her eyes, shielding him from her vision, as she slid the knife into the tomato. Jess itched to brush the strands behind her ear, to follow his fingers with his tongue and lick a trail down the row of gold earrings along her lobe. And then he'd bite her just below her lowest earring, a soft nip that would make her moan for more.

Over the past several days they'd talked in passing, whenever he could get a few moments with her. But he hadn't had a chance to snag her alone since that one night. Jess had been aware of her watching him when he was working out at the corrals, and he'd done his fair share of keeping an eye on her, too.

It'd turned him on to watch her practicing her kickboxing in that storage room she'd converted into a workout center. She'd be one tough little opponent in a fight if she was as good as he thought she was. He liked the way she pitched in around the ranch and helped out wherever she was needed, instead of sitting back and letting everyone else do the work just 'cause she was on vacation. She was a hard worker, good with horses and people, friendly and considerate.

And damn but he had to have her.

Biding his time wasn't Jess's style. When he made up his mind, it was as good as done. It sure it didn't sit well with him, having to wait for Trace to break it off with her boyfriend. Jess needed to claim Trace, and hell if he was going to wait much longer.

The last few days he hadn't had much of a choice in staying away. He'd been so busy following up on leads that were bringing him closer to breaking that drug-smuggling operation wide open. Rick McAllister hadn't been able to get much from Big Tits, but there had been a sighting of Forrester in the vicinity where the cows had been poisoned.

And then the bastard had mailed that threatening note to Dee, and that had really pissed Jess off. He was sure it was Forrester, although he didn't have proof...yet. Jake had taken the card into Customs and had it dusted, but there'd been nothing but Dee's and Trace's prints on it. It was a store bought gag card, and Jake was attempting to track down exactly where it had been sold and then he'd find out if the salesperson recalled who she'd sold it to.

"Hey there, Jess." At the sound of Dee's voice, Trace's head shot up and her cheeks blushed a nice shade of rose as her eyes met his. "You able to join us for dinner tonight, or you heading into town for some Friday night action?" Dee asked.

"Depends." Jess gave Trace a slow smile. "If Trace here is up for dancing, we could head on over to Sierra Vista."

Trace's eyes widened and she blushed a rich shade of red. "I, uh, can't."

"Guess I'll just stay for dinner then." Jess winked then turned his attention to Dee. "Need a hand?"

"You're not flirting with my little sister, now are you?" Dee cocked an eyebrow, the corner of her mouth quirking into a smile. "She's taken, you know."

Jess gave a slow nod as his gaze moved back to Trace. "You're right. This woman belongs to only one man."

And *he* was the man she belonged to.

Dee laughed and gestured with the tortilla she was holding. "You could cut up the onions for Trace. She hates 'em."

At the mention of onions, Trace's freckled nose crinkled and she pointed the knife she was holding at a bunch of green onions on the granite countertop. "Have at it, big guy."

"Sure thing." Jess ambled over to the sink and washed his hands. Trace kept her attention focused on the tomato, dicing it into the smallest bits he'd ever seen. "You aiming to turn that into sauce?"

Trace's cheeks burned as she stopped in mid-chop and stared down at the desecrated tomatoes. "I, uh, like them that way," she said as she lifted the cutting board and scraped the tomato goop into a bowl with the knife. Darned if she was going to tell Jess that she'd been daydreaming about him the whole time she was dicing the tomato. He was all she'd been thinking about, every darn minute, since that night at the hot tub.

"How would you like to join us for dinner tomorrow night, Jess?" Dee asked from behind them. "Catie and Jarrod are joining us and we're playing poker afterwards. You'd make it an even six."

Trace's gaze shot up to meet Jess's and he grinned. "Strip poker?" he said with a teasing glint in his eyes and Dee laughed. "Count me in."

"Just be prepared to ante up, cowboy." Dee banged the frying pan against a burner as she moved it off the heat. "And keep your clothes on."

Jess chuckled and gave Trace a look that said he could see right through her blouse. Her body ached so badly for him she could hardly stand it.

"I'm finished with the taco shells," Dee said, and Trace glanced back over her shoulder to see her sister shut off the stovetop burner. "I'll let Jake know dinner's about ready," Dee added. "Back in a sec."

The moment she left the kitchen, Jess moved close to Trace, his jean clad thighs brushing against her as he murmured, "Have you told him?"

Jess's spicy aftershave flowed over Trace, bringing back memories of the Christmas party and of the hot tub, making it difficult to concentrate on his words. She slipped the vegetable knife into the dishwasher and furrowed her brow, barely able to think with him so close. "Ah…told who about what?" she said as she shut the dishwasher door.

He caught her chin in his hand, forcing her to look at him. His touch caused her skin to tingle and her nipples to peak beneath her blouse.

"Your ex," he said, his blue eyes intent. "About us."

"Ex…um…" Trace could scarcely breathe the way Jess was looking at her. "You mean Harold?"

His smile was tight. "Unless you've got any other boyfriends I need to know about."

Trace thought about telling Jess that he sure as hell assumed a lot. That it was none of his business what she told Harold. That there was no 'us.'

But instead she could only think about how badly she wanted to slide her fingers into the thick brown hair beneath his cowboy hat. How she wanted to see his incredible body again, how she wanted to touch him and taste him…to feel his cock deep inside her.

Cripes but she had it bad.

Lust. A serious case of cowboy lust.

Jess's smile turned sensual as he ran his thumb along her lower lip. "I can read those pretty green eyes, sugar. We're right for one another, but for some crazy reason you're fighting it."

"You don't know that," she whispered.

"It's the truth." Jess lowered his head, bringing his mouth inches above hers. "You're flat out too scared to admit it."

Trace pressed her palms against his chest and almost groaned out loud. She could feel the play of his powerful muscles beneath his western shirt.

"I—I barely know you," she finally said.

"Sugar, we already know each other better than some folks who've been together for years."

She shook her head. "We only met a week ago."

"Doesn't matter." He brought his face closer and filled all her senses with his presence. She felt as though she was drowning, losing herself in this virile man, and *wanting* to lose herself in him.

The sound of Dee's and Jake's voices snapped Trace out of her Jess-induced trance. Pulling free of his grip, she grabbed the bowl of tomatoes and dodged to the other side of the kitchen just as her sister and brother-in-law entered the room. Jess's soft chuckle punctuated the pounding of her heart and she didn't know whether to fling the whole bowl of diced tomatoes at him, or throw herself into his arms.

Chapter Seven

Jess moved beside Trace as she dug out the playing cards from the china cabinet drawer, and she shivered from his nearness. The light cotton dress she was wearing suddenly felt too thin, made her feel too vulnerable, like she was wearing nothing around him.

All evening last night at dinner, and then again tonight, Jess had taken every opportunity to brush against her, to touch her when no one was looking.

"What are we playing?" Catie asked from behind Trace just as she finally located the cards.

"How about five card stud?" Jess suggested, the warmth of his breath caressing her ear.

"Sounds as good as any," Jarrod said as Trace slipped past Jess and tossed the deck onto the dinner table. Jake had removed the two middle table leaves a few minutes earlier, so that the table was much smaller and cozier for playing poker. Now instead of a long oblong table, it was almost circular.

Catie's blonde hair bounced against her shoulders as she plopped herself in Jarrod's lap. She wrapped her arms around his neck and nuzzled his mustache. "You ready for me to kick your ass, Sheriff?"

"Now this I gotta see." Jake pulled a chair up to the table, his gray eyes glinting with humor as he grabbed the deck of cards. "But you're gonna have to find a seat of your own, Cat."

"Watch it, Reynolds." Catie gave Jake a mock glare then kissed Jarrod before getting to her feet and slipping into the chair next to her husband.

Dee carried in a tray from the kitchen, filled with bowls of pretzels, bottles of beer and wine, along with wineglasses. Blue followed at Dee's heels, and then settled himself under her chair, his head on his paws.

Trace helped her sister, and after everything was distributed, she took her seat next to Jess, who was dealing out stacks of red, white, and blue poker chips. When she eased into her chair, he paused and gave her that dark, sexy look that made her clit ache. She had no idea how she was going to make it through this night without having him.

Maybe Jess was right. Maybe she should call Harold and tell him it was over.

Why did she keep putting it off?

Because I'm afraid…afraid that I could lose my heart to this cowboy.

Trace sighed and took a long sip of her zinfandel, letting the liquid slide down her throat until it warmed her belly. She could feel Jess's eyes on her, but she refused to look at him. Every time those blue eyes met hers, she forgot about all the reasons why it wouldn't work with him…because of her career and her home in England.

Jake finished shuffling the deck. "Deuces are wild," he said as he dealt each player five cards, the first two face down and the other three face up.

Catie and Dee chatted about the new shooting range that had been opened up several miles west of Douglas, while Trace watched Jake deal the cards. So odd that he was her brother-in-law now. And how nice and comfortable it felt with all six of them having dinner together and playing cards.

Like, maybe she could get used to this.

The longer she was away from Harold, the more she felt that their relationship was not completely open and sincere. With Harold she never knew what he was thinking, what secrets he kept hidden away from her behind that perplexing brown gaze. And she finally realized that he kept his emotions too tightly contained. Somewhere inside him there was a passionate man, but she'd never seen that side of him. And as good of a boxer as she'd heard he'd been in his youth, there was no way he could have been as unemotional as he was now. Something had to have happened a long time ago to have made him shut off that part of him.

But with Jess…yeah, there was lots of mystery in the man, but she knew exactly where she stood with him. He wanted her.

And damn but she wanted him.

It was time…she needed to call Harold. Maybe nothing would come of her relationship with Jess, but she didn't want to look back and wish she'd done things differently.

"You heading home for Christmas, Jess?" Dee asked as she looked over her cards. "Hey, no peeking," she added to Jake with a frown as he leaned back in his chair as though he might look at her cards.

Jess gave a non-committal shrug as he discarded one card and drew another. He was deep enough undercover that if a search was done on him, it would come up that he was born and raised in Cheyenne, Wyoming, and had studied agribusiness at Auburn University.

Truth of the matter was that he'd lived on a ranch outside Houston his entire life before heading off to the University of Texas to earn his bachelor's in Criminal Justice and then going into the academy.

He wondered what Trace would think once she learned that he wasn't who she thought he was. Well, he'd just have to cross that cattle guard when he came to it.

"You don't have any place to go for Christmas?" Trace asked after she tossed a card onto the discard pile. Her green eyes were wide, as though she felt concerned that he'd be alone over the holidays.

He smiled as his gaze met hers. Wouldn't hurt to tell a bit of the truth. "If I don't show up Christmas Day for some of my mama's roasted turkey, cornbread stuffing, and her special pecan pie, she'll never forgive me."

"And I'll bet you'd never disappoint her," Trace said softly, looked to the cards in her hand. "You have any brothers or sisters?"

"Two of each." He grinned at the thought of his big, loving family. "And between all of them, damn near a dozen nieces and nephews. Miss them all like hell."

Her eyebrows raised in surprise. "I can't imagine having such a big family." She gestured toward her sister with one of her cards. "It's always been just Dee and me. Our mom died when we were pretty young, and then our dad might as well have been in another state once she passed away."

"That's the truth." Dee nodded. "It's your turn, Lawless."

He studied his cards. Two pair, not too bad. "I'll hold."

"You're from Texas, aren't you?" Trace asked.

He raised an eyebrow. "Why do you say that?"

"Your drawl." Her eyes focused on Jess. "It's very Texan."

The woman certainly had a good ear.

"Is something going on between you two that we ought to know about?" Catie interrupted in her usual direct manner. "It's your play, Trace."

Saved by the wildcat. Jess smiled as Trace's cheeks flushed again and she studied her cards.

"I'll hold. I think." She frowned and looked at them again. "Yes, I'll hold."

Before Trace had the chance to repeat her question about his accent, Jake asked Jess something about Imp, that spoiled-rotten bull of Dee's.

As the night progressed, and more beer and wine had been consumed, the whole evening seemed to take on a surreal feel to Trace. No one seemed to notice the times that Jess would deliberately brush her breast with his hand, or lean close to whisper in her ear.

And then Jess slipped one hand under the table and caressed her thigh.

She froze, her gaze locked on her cards. Afraid to move and afraid to make a sound, like someone at the table might notice that Jess's hand was creeping up the inside of her thigh under her dress, nearing her mound. Even though everyone seemed wrapped up in the poker game, or tipsy from the alcohol, how could they not notice that Jess only had one hand on the tabletop?

Yet she couldn't get herself to make him stop.

While play continued, the chatter around the table was nothing more than a loud buzzing noise to Trace's ears. She stared at her cards, not seeing them at all as Jess's finger reached the soaked crotch of her panties. If anyone had asked her at that moment what she had in her hand, she wouldn't have been able to name the cards. No matter that she was staring right at them.

Jess slid his fingers inside the elastic, and touched the soft curls of her pussy, and she almost closed her eyes. Oh, jeez. She had to make him stop.

Mindlessly she tried to play the poker game as his finger entered her creamy wetness and he stroked her clit. If it wasn't for Jess whispering suggestions throughout each hand, she would have lost everything within moments.

She could smell his flesh, could smell her own arousal. Could everyone else smell it, too?

The sensations in her abdomen grew stronger and tighter, and she knew she was close to climax. "You can't scream," Jess whispered in her ear. "When you come, you're gonna have to hold it in, sugar."

Trace bit down hard on her lower lip as the orgasm took hold of her body and shook it like a mesquite tree in a summer storm. She braced her hand on her forehead and looked down, shielding her face from everyone at the table as her body trembled, and Jess's finger drew the climax out even longer.

"You all right, Trace?" Dee asked through Trace's alcohol and orgasm haze.

Jess slipped his hand out of Trace's panties and she fought to control her breathing, to let her heart rate slow to a normal pace.

"Too much wine," Trace mumbled and rubbed her temples with her thumb and forefinger. "I think I'm done for."

Jess chuckled and murmured so that only she could hear, "Like I've already told you, we haven't even started yet, sugar."

* * * * *

Trace tossed and turned in her bed, slipping in and out of a misty dream world.

The poker game went on and on, like it was never going to end.

And then she was on her back on the table, her dress hiked up around her waist and Jess sliding his cock deep into her pussy.

Everyone continued playing around them, tossing their now rainbow-colored poker chips onto Trace's bare belly. Even as Jess fucked her, she realized the poker chips on her belly were actually condoms. Lots and lots of condoms across her stomach and scattered across the table, but Jess hadn't put one on.

He kept driving into her, the game around them never stopping. Dee and Catie repeated something that sounded like poison, poison, *while Jake and Jarrod responded with* fire, fire.

All Trace knew was that she needed to come so bad she couldn't stand it. But the tension in her abdomen only intensified until she thought she'd lose her mind...

And then she was alone.

Utterly and completely alone. Standing somewhere dark and cold, like a cave, and she was entirely naked.

Where was Jess? Without him she felt incomplete, lonely even.

Trace didn't know what had happened, or where she was, but something in her gut suddenly told her that Dee was in danger.

She had to find her sister. Had to help her.

And then Trace was out in the open. She ran across the dream desert...she dodged through tumbleweeds and mesquite bushes, hurrying toward the barn. Yes, that was it. She had to get to the barn. She had to hurry —

Trace's eyes flew open and she stared up at the white canopy above her bed. Her heart raced like she'd really been running and she couldn't catch her breath.

Her limbs trembled as she sat up in bed and braced her back against the headboard and her arms on her knees. That horrible feeling that something was wrong wouldn't go away. She'd never been superstitious. Never been one to believe in dreams or intuition, but she couldn't shake the feeling that she should get up and go check on things. Why, she didn't know, but she just had to do it.

A sense of urgency took over. She hurried out of bed, pulled her nightgown over her head and tossed it onto a chair. After she yanked on her sweatpants and an oversized t-shirt, she stuffed her feet into her Nikes. She grabbed her jacket as she headed down the hall and toward the front door.

Someone had left on the Christmas lights, and they helped her make her way without stumbling. Blue stirred in the kitchen and Trace heard the dog's nails click against the tile as he followed her into the living room.

"You sense it to, don't you, boy?" Trace murmured as she neared the window.

Blue's ears pricked forward as he jumped up and rested his front paws on the windowsill and looked out into the night with Trace.

Everything was still. Nothing moved.

And then Blue growled.

Trace was about to look at him when she thought she saw a flicker at the far end of the barn, where the storage room was, and her skin chilled. There it was. Stronger now. Like a flashlight…but different.

Her heart pounded and she started to yell for Jake and Dee, that there was an intruder, when she realized what the flicker was.

Fire.

Blue growled and then barked, loud and sharp, and Trace shouted at the top of her lungs, "Fire in the barn! Fire in the barn!"

She ran toward their bedroom door, still yelling, but as she reached it Jake came crashing out, pulling on his boots, his pants undone and no shirt on.

"A fire in the barn," Trace repeated frantically and then turned and ran for the front door, yanking it open and barreling into the night, screaming, "Fire! Fire!"

Blue barked at her heels and Trace didn't stop yelling as she ran toward the barn. Vaguely she remembered seeing the man's shadow from the house's window, but she couldn't be concerned with that now. There were too many animals locked up in that barn and she had to help get them out.

The acrid odor of smoke met her as she neared the barn. She coughed and choked as she tried to shout some more. The bell! Trace dove for the ancient bell and grabbed the rope hanging down from it and pulled.

It started clanging, loud and clear in the night. Above the noise she could already hear the shouts of men and saw them running toward the barn.

Smoke poured from the barn and the horses screamed their fright from inside. She'd seen the fire at the opposite end of the barn, and so far no flames from the barn door.

Trace released the bell's rope and dove for the lights, flooding the barn with a yellow glow that blinded her for a second. She yanked off her jacket and tied the arms around her head so that her nose and mouth were covered, but she could still see. Dodging inside the barn, she ran toward Dancer's stall.

Men shouted behind her, and Trace thought she heard someone calling her name, but she didn't care about anything except getting those animals out.

Smoke burned her eyes as she reached Dancer. The mare was wild-eyed and frantically pawing at the stall door. Trace climbed up the side of the gate, took the jacket from her face and covered Dancer's eyes with it before releasing the bolt lock, speaking to the mare in low, steady tones and calming her down.

As she led Dancer out of the barn, the smell of smoke nearly overwhelmed her. She heard shouts, saw men rushing back and forth, and knew they were fighting the fire. Everything seemed to be a blur, a horrific kaleidoscope of sights, sounds, smells and sensation.

When she finally made it out of the barn with Dancer, Trace led the horse to the closest corral. The teenaged ranch hand helped her open the gate and put the mare safely inside. Clenching her jacket in her hands, Trace rushed back to the barn, set to go in again.

Someone grabbed her from behind and whirled her around. "What the hell are you doing?" Jess's face was streaked with smoke his furious glare focused on her.

"I'm getting the animals out!" She tried to pull away, but he wouldn't let her go.

"It's too damn dangerous in there, you little shit." Jess gripped her arm and started dragging her toward the far end of the barn. "That smoke could kill you," he said as he brought her to where the men were fighting the fire with hoses and buckets and fire extinguishers. A sigh of relief rushed through her when she realized the fire was almost out.

"Get a bucket and help from this end," he said in a tone she'd never heard from him before. "If you try to go into that barn before I say it's time, I'll tie you to the fence post."

With that he strode back to where the men where still throwing buckets of water on the fire from the stock tanks, and spraying it down with the hose. Trace's first instinct was to be furious with him for his high-handedness, but then she realized what it was she'd heard in his tone and seen in his eyes.

He'd been scared for her. Afraid something had happened, or that something would happen to her.

If she'd thought it was all a blur before, it seemed even more so, later. By the time the fire was completely out and all the animals treated and returned to their stalls, dawn was breaking. Trace was so tired that she could hardly see straight. Her muscles ached, her eyes and throat burned and she felt like she'd sleep for a week.

While the men had fought the fire, Dee had called the sheriff's office. Jarrod had arrived by the time the fire was out, and spent time going over the scene with Jake and Jess.

After they took a look around, the three men were sure the fire had been deliberately set. And when Trace told them about the shadow she'd seen, that confirmed it in their eyes, although they intended to investigate it further.

Even as her tired mind listened to the men discuss the fire, it sure seemed like Jess knew a lot more about crime investigations than most ranch foreman would probably know.

Trace could hardly keep her eyes open, and she didn't protest when Jess insisted she get back to the house, take a shower and then get to bed. He didn't say another word about her running into the barn like she had. Instead he escorted her into the house, kissed the top of her head, and then left her there staring out the living room window and watching him walk away.

Chapter Eight

Jess stood behind Trace at the firing range as she aimed the handgun at the target. "That's it, sugar," he murmured, even though she couldn't hear him through the protective ear coverings she wore, "you're doing fine."

She seemed to understand him, though, and her hands were steadier on this shot than they'd been during her first half dozen. Trace had argued with him about not needing to learn how to handle a firearm, but after that threatening note and then the incident in the barn just a couple of nights ago, he wasn't taking any chances.

Someone was messing around with the MacLeod women, and he was going to make sure nothing happened to either of them.

When Trace finished firing that last round of bullets, she set the gun down, pulled off her ear coverings and gave him a tired smile. "I think I did better that time."

Jess nodded and pressed the button that slowly brought the target back to them. "I think you're right," he said as he pulled the target off the clip. She had a tendency to aim a little high, most of her shots going to the target's neck, but it was a sight better than her first try. Those holes had been scattered all over the target.

Trace rubbed the earrings along her left ear, something he noticed she did whenever she was deep in thought. "I don't understand why this person would do the things he's doing? Why the note? Why burn the barn?"

With a shrug, Jess replied, "I don't know, but I aim to find out." Best he could do without getting into more privileged information. Truth was he had a pretty good idea, and he knew he was getting closer to finding the bastards responsible.

Frowning, Trace looked as though she intended to say something else when she turned to look at the shooter setting up right beside them. Big Tits Newman herself.

Trace turned away and started packing up the ammo, and then slid the gun back into its zippered case.

"Won't do you a damn bit of good in there." Jess smiled and rubbed his hand over her back. "You need to carry it around. Get the feel of it."

"It makes me nervous." Trace eased the zipper up and around the case. "I feel safer using my bare fists and my feet."

"You're real good at it, too." He moved his fingers to her neck and she shivered beneath his touch. "I'd wager you could kick some ass if you had the chance."

She raised her brows. "So...you've watched me practice my kickboxing?"

"Every chance I get," he murmured.

A commotion in the lane next to them caught Jess's attention and he turned his gaze toward Kathy Newman's target that she'd just pulled in.

"Wow," Trace said, a touch of surprise in her voice. "She's really good."

He shrugged as he studied her target. The shots were all centered on the head. Apparently Newman liked the idea of blowing a man's brains out better than his heart.

When Jess and Trace moved to pass the woman, Big Tits practically shoved her shot-up target in Trace's face. Her smile was as thickly sweet as her perfume. "A hell of a lot better than your pitiful display," she said.

With more class than Kathy Newman could ever hope to have, Trace nodded. "You're absolutely right. I could never be like you, Kathy."

Big Tits gave a smug smile and turned back to her next target, clearly dismissing Jess and Trace.

Jess draped his arm around Trace's shoulders as they headed out to his old Chevy. "You make that call to Harold yet?" he asked.

* * * * *

Three days later, Trace glared at the punching bag Jake had set up in a corner of the barn storage room, where she'd trained every day for almost two weeks now. The difference now was the heavy odor of smoke from the fire that just wouldn't go away.

Her breath came in angry huffs and sweat trickled down the small of her back beneath her workout clothes. Her skin was warm and flushed from her intense workout, and she barely felt the chill in the air.

Damn those bastards, Trace fumed at those who were responsible for the fire six days ago and for the dozen cattle that had been poisoned last night—found dead this morning. She jabbed at the leather bag several times, a litany of *damn them, damn them, damn them* running through her mind with every punch.

Using skill obtained from four years of kickboxing practice, Trace raised one leg, and with a powerful side kick she slammed her Nike clad foot into the punching bag. Her ponytail slapped against her back as she followed up with five quick bare-fisted jabs, each punch feeling solid and good, and relieving some of her frustration.

A little, anyway.

Part of her frustration was sexual, and no amount of punching *or* masturbating was going to make *that* ache go away. Nothing and no one could — except Jess.

Within moments of meeting him, the cowboy had turned Trace's perfect world upside down. She had an incredible job, a great boyfriend, and *had* been genuinely happy with her life. Maybe slightly bored with Harold, but she'd figured that was normal in a long-term relationship. She'd thought that she had everything that she needed or wanted.

But ever since she'd met Jess, no matter how hard Trace tried, she hadn't been able to stop thinking about him. Hadn't been able to stop *wanting* him. And darn it, she'd *tried*.

If she wasn't careful she was going to wind up falling in love with the cowboy, and that just didn't fit into her plans.

Trace finally had gotten the courage to call Harold, to tell him that it was over, but he hadn't been there when she'd called, and hadn't returned her messages. If it was possible, she'd rather tell him in person, but she didn't want him to come all the way out to Arizona for Christmas, just to have her dump him. She'd called him every day since that morning out at the shooting range with Jess. Maybe she didn't know what would happen in the future with Jess or any other man, but she knew it was time to quit avoiding ending things with Harold.

She gave the black leather punching bag another wallop.

It was definitely time to let Jess give her what he'd been offering. Just thinking about the man made Trace's nipples ache, her pussy tingle, and drenched her panties.

Damn but she wanted him.

Argh.

In a quick movement, Trace spun and kicked the punching bag dead-on with her right foot. In a flash she nailed it again with her left foot, then jabbed at the bag with each fist in rapid-fire succession.

Just as she was about to kick the bag again, hair prickled at her nape.

Strong hands gripped her shoulders from behind.

Wild thoughts tore through her mind — of the arsonist and the bastards who'd poisoned the cattle.

Adrenalin pumped through Trace, and she went on defensive auto-pilot.

She shot out her foot, low and hard, connecting with a booted shin. At the same time she twisted and broke free of the grip on her shoulders. She whirled, sending her fist into a hard muscled abdomen —

A fraction of a second before she realized it was Jess.

"You've got a helluva left, sugar." He grimaced and rubbed his abs with his palm. "That's certainly one way to greet a man."

"Oops." Trace's cheeks burned as she tossed her ponytail over her shoulder. "Maybe that'll teach you not to sneak up on a woman."

He took a step closer, dominating her personal space, but she lifted her chin and held her ground. Beneath his dark Stetson, dirt streaked his stubbled face and he smelled of dust, horse, and testosterone. Sweat soaked his blue denim work shirt, and dang if he wasn't wearing a pair of well broken-in chaps.

No fair. A good looking cowboy in chaps had always been one of her weaknesses. There was just something sexy about a man in all that leather.

Trace shivered, her nipples hardening, her pussy throbbing and tingling. She could picture him naked, with only his chaps on, his cock thrusting out—

Jess's wicked blue eyes glittered as he moved so close that his belt buckle brushed her belly. "I've been dying to get you alone." He placed one hand on her hip and reached up to trail his thumb along her cheekbone with his other. "I can't hardly sleep at night, picturing you in my bed. Thinking about sliding between those silky thighs and fucking you."

Heat suffused her body, starting from where his hand rested on her hip, flowing through her pussy, up to her breasts and neck and on up to the roots of her hair.

Trace swallowed hard past the dry lump in her throat. She licked her lips and a muscle in his jaw twitched. God but she wanted him to kiss her. Wanted to feel his sweaty naked body against her own.

His mouth neared hers and she braced her hands against his muscled chest. "Did you tell him?" he asked, the deep rumble of his words rolling through her body like thunder.

"I—I haven't been able to reach Harold," she whispered.

"Bullshit." Jess slid his hand from her cheekbone, roughly brushing her earrings as he reached for her hair.

Grabbing her ponytail in his fist, he pulled on it, gently bringing her closer to him. He swept his lips over hers and she tasted his breath as she moaned. He nipped at her lower lip and she sighed into his mouth. "I can't hold off much longer. Get a hold of your ex and break the news."

"Tracilynn?" A British man's voice called from the other end of the barn, shattering the hold Jess had on Trace. "Are you in here?"

"Oh, God. It's Harold." Trace tried to push away from Jess but he kept his grip on her hip and her ponytail. "Let me go!"

Jess's eyes narrowed, and his voice was firm as he said, "Looks like you'll have your chance to break it to him now."

Chapter Nine

Shock coursed through Trace's veins. *Harold?* What was he doing here? He wasn't supposed to arrive for a week yet. She couldn't let him find out this way — with her in another man's arms.

Trace braced her hands against Jess's powerful chest and pushed. He held onto her ponytail for a moment longer, then let it slide through his fingers as she broke away from him.

She couldn't seem to break eye contact with him, even though she needed to go talk with Harold. Trace had never felt so sexy, so attractive, and so secure as she did around Jess — while totally unbalanced all at once.

He was driving her crazy.

"Tracilynn?" Harold called again.

"Coming," she shouted as she grabbed her sweat jacket from a hook on the wall and slipped it on.

Trace started to leave, then paused and looked back to Jess. With that possessive look on his face she could just imagine him pulling a Neanderthal routine and getting in the middle of things. She pointed her finger at him. "You — you behave," she whispered before turning on her heel. She jogged around the corner and spotted Harold at the opposite end of the barn.

Trace came to a dead stop, unable to make herself hurry toward the man she'd been with for the last two years of her life.

It had been almost three weeks since she'd kissed Harold goodbye at Heathrow Airport in London. A light, conservative kiss since he was a typical reserved English gentleman who never indulged in public displays of affection.

But when she saw him there, in the world she'd grown up in, it was almost like the last two years had happened to another woman. No excitement rushed through her at the sight of him, no fluttering of anticipation in her belly. Just a pleasant feeling of seeing a good friend…mixed with the twinge of uncertainty and a distant ache over not wanting to hurt someone she truly cared about. And guilt, too, for not remaining true to their relationship. She was a one-man woman all right, it just turned out that Harold wasn't that man.

"There you are, my dear." Harold smiled as he strolled up to Trace. Yes, he was a devastatingly handsome man, fit and well muscled, and about as tall as Jess. His high cheekbones gave him an aristocratic look, but his sandy blond hair and deep brown eyes made him friendly and approachable, and definitely gorgeous and sexy.

Harold's cobalt blue polo shirt, khaki slacks, and brown loafers were glaringly out of place in the barn, but she couldn't imagine the sophisticated and refined man in anything more casual. Funny, but she'd never seen him in a pair of jeans. As far as she knew, he didn't even own any.

"I expected you next week," Trace said as he reached her and took both of her hands in his.

"A surprise, dearest." Harold lowered his head and gave her a light kiss. His lips were cool and firm, and he smelled of the musk cologne she had given him for Christmas last year.

As he touched her, she felt nothing. Nothing at all.

"I couldn't be more astonished." Trace did her best to smile as Harold drew back.

It occurred to her that she was sweaty, her hair poking out of her ponytail, and her face probably streaked with dirt from her intense workout. A part of her couldn't help but analyze the difference between Harold's greeting and Jess's. Even though she looked like a mess, Jess had made her feel beautiful, sensual, and wanted. If he'd had the chance, she knew Jess would fuck her right there in the barn.

On the other hand, Harold probably would prefer she took a shower before they slipped into bed together. And he would definitely never call sex *fucking.* For that matter he'd never call his penis a *cock*, or her vulva a *pussy.* He was too *reserved.*

And Trace, well, she liked the forbidden words. They were hard and erotic, and they excited her. She wanted to be fucked by a man who loved her, a man she loved in return. A man who didn't hold any part of himself back from her.

She cared about Harold—cared a lot. He was like a pair of shoes she enjoyed wearing, just because they were comfortable.

But there wasn't any doubt left in her mind at all. She wasn't in love with Harold, and she truly never had been.

When the Englishman kissed Trace, Jess gritted his teeth and clenched his fists. He had to fight the urge to grab the bastard by his collar and kick his pansy ass back to where he'd come from.

Trace was Jess's woman now. If Harold didn't back off, Jess was going to have to get in the middle of things in a hurry. He strode toward them as the man drew away from the kiss. Before Jess reached them, Trace said something he couldn't hear and Harold smiled.

Just as Jess came up behind Trace, the Englishmen glanced at him. "Hullo," he said as he released Trace and held out his hand to Jess. "Harold St. John. And you must be one of the, er, cattle herders?"

"Something like that." Jess shook the man's hand, surprised by his equally firm grip. "Jess Lawless."

"He's the Flying M's foreman," Trace said in a rush as her gaze darted from Harold to Jess and back. "He, ah, works for Dee."

"You two have some talking to do." Jess's eyes rested on Trace, telling her without words that he expected her to do what he knew her heart had to be telling her all along. "I'll be out at the corrals if you need me."

He gave Harold a nod and touched his hand to his Stetson, then strode out of the barn without looking back. His gut clenched and it was all he could do not to turn around, grab that woman, and cart her off by her ponytail like a damned caveman.

Trace watched Jess walk away, his leather chaps framing his tight ass as he headed out the barn door. Dang but a cowboy in chaps made her hot. Although Jess definitely made her hotter than any man *ever* had — chaps, or no chaps.

"Would you like to freshen up, my dear?" Harold asked, and she caught the note of concern in his voice.

Trace snapped her gaze from Jess's retreating backside and met Harold's warm brown eyes. He was so kind, gentle and considerate. Everything that Jess wasn't.

Although that wasn't quite true. Jess had been considerate in his own way—he was giving her space to talk with Harold, for one thing. And Jess hadn't taken advantage of her when he could have that night in the hot tub. Heck, she'd been ready to screw his brains out right then and there.

The mere thought of Jess's cock plunging deep inside her aching pussy made her wet with sweat. And with the heat rushing to her face, she was sure she'd turned as red as an Arizona sunset.

How could she have such graphic thoughts in front of Harold?

He frowned, his brows furrowing. The concern made him look all the more regal and distant. "Tracilynn, are you quite all right?"

She clasped her hands together and squeezed them so tightly her knuckles ached. "I tried to call you, but you must have been on your way," she said so fast she stumbled over the words. "I—I should have called sooner, but I wasn't certain. Or maybe it's just that I wasn't sure how to tell you."

Harold's eyes held hers as he slid his hand into a pocket of his slacks. Sparkles flashed in the barn's dim interior when he brought out a diamond ring and held it on his palm. "Tell me I'm not too late," he said softly, the rich timbre of his accent lending the plea a special poignancy.

Trace bit the inside of her lip as the diamond flashed and glittered. It had to be over a carat—and the band was probably platinum. Harold would choose such a symbol, a concrete statement of her worth—and his.

Emotions rolled through her like bouncing tumbleweeds. She had never come so close to having every material thing she'd ever wanted. Not to mention the one thing she'd never had in her childhood: an even-tempered, safe, dependable man.

In a handful of days, after a few blistering encounters with a stranger, was she truly ready to throw away such security?

Harold stood before her, holding his ring, clinging to his hopeful expression even as his eyes hinted that he knew the truth. Trace saw him completely in the prismatic diamond light: a wonderful, kind, and passionless prison of a man.

Regret flooded her.

She knew what she needed, and it wasn't safety or propriety.

No.

Her future lay in risk, in leather, in the desert heat, and a cowboy's muscled arms.

At least for now.

For the first time in her adult life, Trace MacLeod felt a sense of freedom and anticipation for tomorrow. A tomorrow that wasn't studiously mapped or planned, or confined in the squeaky-clean manners of the corporate world.

She had to hurt this man, and that reality shook her deeply. With her emotions turned loose, she felt the sting of his pain even before she inflicted it. No guilt, though. The real wrong would be pretending to love Harold when she didn't. Giving him parts of herself that rightfully belonged to another man.

"I'm sorry, but I can't marry you." With a rattling sigh, she reached up and closed his fingers over the ring. "You're an amazing man, Harold Rockmore St. John. Somewhere there's a woman who'll rock your world."

Harold hesitated. For the first time ever, Trace thought she saw a blaze of pure, raw emotion change the man's features. For a split-second, he seemed younger. Fierce and lion-like.

And just as fast, the look vanished. Harold had tucked his feelings back in their bottomless box. The corner of his mouth quirked in a resigned smile. "You did a lovely job of that. Rejecting me, I mean."

Trace felt her insides coalesce and firm up. She knew she'd made the right decision, and thank God Harold was taking it so well. "Your woman-to-be, I mean she'll *really* rock you. Not just shake you up a little."

Her former lover gave a hint of a smile and slipped the ring into his pocket. His expression told her he was hurt…but at the same time was that relief in his eyes?

But as was his habit, he didn't speak about it any further. The conversation was quite clearly over.

Arm in arm, Trace and Harold walked out of the barn in comfortable silence, making the short trek to his red sports car with a rental sticker on the bumper.

"You're not returning to London," he said as though the statement were fact as they came to a stop next to the driver's side door.

Trace cut her gaze up to meet his and she started to tell him *of course* she was. But instead she said, "I…haven't made any decisions. My life, my career is in England."

"Ah," he placed a light kiss on her forehead. "But your love is here."

"What? No—" Trace's protest was silenced with Harold's finger firmly against her lips.

"It's in your eyes, my dear." He glanced toward the corrals. "And I do believe I saw it in his."

Trace's entire body tingled as she followed the direction of Harold's gaze and saw Jess leaning against the corral's wooden railings. He'd folded his arms across his chest and pulled his Stetson too low for her to see his eyes, but she could make out the hard line of his frown. He was still dressed in his dusty clothes and chaps, and to her he'd never looked better.

She looked back to Harold as he removed his finger from her mouth. With a smile he brushed his lips over hers then pulled back and winked. "And I'm sure that little kiss will put a twist in the chap's knickers. He seems the possessive type, as well he should be with a rare prize like you."

Trace wrapped her arms around Harold's neck and kissed his cheek. He might be wrong about her not returning to London, but he was one heck of a guy. "Watch out for the local girls while you're in Arizona." She released him and stepped back. "That sexy accent of yours is a killer."

Harold smiled as he opened the door to the sports car and climbed in, then shut the door and buzzed the window open. "Dunno about that, my dear. Might have to sample the wares a bit, don't you think? I've always fancied American experiments."

She smiled, feeling almost giddy as the engine roared and he backed the car out of the driveway and headed down the road.

Trace did her best to ignore Jess as she watched Harold drive away, but the cowboy might as well have been right beside her rather than a hundred yards off at the corrals.

Instead she focused on the car's taillights and the growl of its engine growing fainter in the distance. Harold. In a red sports car. Threatening to sample the local wares.

Too funny. Maybe she should give him Nicole's phone number. After all, turnabout was fair play. And Trace had definitely been turned about. Upside down and inside out. Her entire life had changed, and in seconds, it would change even more.

Risk…leather…desert heat…a cowboy's muscled arms.

Her heart hammered, and she shivered in the evening's growing chill. As if to protect herself, she wrapped her jacket tighter.

Who am I kidding? I'm way past protection. Jumped off the damned cliff a few days ago, and so far, I'm still flying.

The sunset seeped across the horizon in hues of orange and purple, and the air smelled crisp and wonderful—of fall in the desert, and winter around the corner. Without looking she knew that Jess was striding toward her. Beneath her jacket her nipples beaded and ached, and a whole swarm of butterflies invaded her belly. Her skin tingled from her scalp to her toes and she felt alive in a way she never had before.

The moment Jess reached her, Trace whirled around to look up at him, a sense of breathless anticipation soaring through her. His eyes were still shadowed by his Stetson, but the tenseness of his jaw and the firm set of his mouth told her that Harold's little show hadn't settled well with her cowboy.

"Well?" Jess demanded, still just as gritty and sweaty as before.

Dang but she had to have him.

"I want to have a word with you," she murmured and turned on her heel before he had a chance to respond. She could feel the heat of his gaze on the sway of her hips, on the curve of her ass, almost as though he was touching her with those strong, calloused hands.

When she was in the shadows of the barn's dusty interior she turned and saw Jess still standing right where she'd left him. She raised her hand and curled her forefinger towards herself, telling him to *"Come and get me,"* with just that little motion and a teasing grin.

His long legs ate up the ground so fast it made her heart beat like thunder, the sound filling her ears. When he was close enough, Trace didn't think twice. She flung her arms around Jess's neck, climbed him like a tree, and wrapped her legs around his hips.

A sensual grin curved his mouth as he cupped her ass and held her tight to him. She felt his leather chaps through the thin material of her sweatpants as he pressed his erection against her pussy.

"I told him." Hunger and need surged through Trace and she brought her mouth to his in a hard rush, a kiss that demanded he give her everything he'd promised and more. "I'm free," she murmured as she bit Jess's lower lip as he'd done to her, letting him feel the depth of her desire for him, her need. "I want you, Jess. I *need* you."

"You're not free." Jess kissed her back, fierce and uncivilized. "You're mine."

His? Fear touched her—fear of the unknown. Fear of losing her heart and soul to this six-foot-one hunk of sex in boots. But for now she wasn't going to think about that. She needed all the wild passion that only Jess could give her.

Holding her tighter yet, Jess groaned and thrust his tongue into her mouth, then pulled away and looked into her eyes. "I've got to have you," he said, his voice rough and filled with need so tangible that she felt the vibrations straight to her core.

Trace kissed the corner of his mouth, his stubble rough against her lips, causing them to tingle. "I want you to fuck me, Jess Lawless."

A rumble rose in his chest, a sound of overwhelming need. "We'll take my truck and head away from here."

"No." She moved her mouth closer to his ear and darted her tongue along his lobe, tasting the salt of his skin. "The barn office. Right now."

Chapter Ten

Jess didn't have to be told twice. He was done waiting. Trace clung to him as he strode toward the office at the end of the barn. She nipped at his earlobe with wild little bites, making those purring sounds that about drove him insane with lust.

When he reached the office, Jess yanked the door open with one hand and slammed it closed behind him. He took Trace straight to the old fashioned desk, sat her down on one end and eased her arms from around his neck and her legs from his waist. He kept his hips pressed tight between her thighs, though. That much ground he wouldn't surrender yet. Not until she was good and ready for him.

Even in the dim light coming through a part in the gingham curtains, he saw how heavily she was breathing and that her nipples were hard enough to raise the fabric of her light jacket.

She reached for his belt, her small hands brushing against his hard cock as she unfastened the buckle. "I need you so bad."

"Hold on." Jess reached over Trace to flip on the desk lamp so that the glow illuminated her beautiful face. In a quick movement he grabbed her lapels and jerked her jacket down to her elbows so that her arms were trapped at her sides.

Her eyes darted to his and she ran her tongue along her lower lip, her eyes dark with passion. "What are you doing?"

"Sit tight." In a matter of seconds he had her shoes and socks off and then reached up to grab her sweatpants at the waistband. "Lift your hips."

Trace obeyed, excitement and arousal swirling through her at such a mad pace that she could barely stand waiting. Cool air rushed against her skin as he stripped away her panties and the sweatpants, leaving her naked from the waist down, open and vulnerable.

"Damn." Jess sucked in his breath as he ran his finger along the soft hair bordering her slit. "You've got the prettiest pussy."

Shivers coursed her spine. "Hurry, Jess." She tried to move, but her arms were still bound by the jacket.

"We'll get there." He pulled apart the snaps of his western work shirt, yanked it off and tossed it aside.

The sight of his chest, the light dusting of dark hair and the powerful muscles, just about undid her. "Hurry," she begged again.

"Double damn," Jess murmured as he pushed her t-shirt up and then pulled down on the lacy cups of her bra, releasing her breasts, yet leaving them pointing high and out. "A pair of fine nipples on the most beautiful breasts I've ever had the pleasure of tasting."

He reached up with one hand take off his hat. "Wait," Trace said and his eyes met hers. "Fuck me with your cowboy hat on." Her gaze dropped to the bulge at his crotch, and the chaps that framed his hips so well. "Leave those on, too."

Jess's smile was so carnal she knew it had to be outlawed in at least half a dozen states. He slid his belt out from the loops and tossed it on the desk beside her, the metal buckle clattering on the polished wood. After releasing the single button on his jeans and unzipping them, he freed his incredible erection. Trace's mouth watered and her pussy was so wet she could feel her juices sliding down to the crack of her ass.

He palmed his cock and moved his hand up and down its awesome length. "You ready for me to fuck you?"

Spreading her legs wider, Trace arched her back, raising her breasts up to him. "If you don't get inside me now, I'm going to scream."

"Oh, I aim to make you scream, plenty." Bracing one of his palms on her thigh, Jess moved between her legs. The feel of his leather chaps along the soft skin of her thighs, and the sight of his erection jutting toward her was such a turn on that she could hardly keep from shouting for him to get inside her.

Jess rubbed the head of his cock up and down her slick pussy lips, teasing her clit with slow, sensuous strokes. Trace gasped at the incredible sensation, unable to believe how close she was to coming, and he'd barely touched her.

"I want to make something real clear." Jess's deep blue gaze locked on her as he continued to tease her by rubbing his erection against her clit. "You're gonna watch me take you. And when I slide into you, sugar, you're mine. No more bullshit, no big city games, and no arguments. I'm staking my claim, for now. Maybe for always."

At that moment that whole darn barn could've been burning down and Trace wouldn't have noticed. Her lips parted, and even with Jess's cock so close to sliding into her, she tried to find a way to deny him, to tell him that she wasn't a possession to claim.

But he had some kind of power over her. A way of making her feel like she was an exquisite treasure he'd discovered, that he would cherish her always — but first he would insist that she give him everything...

Her body, her soul, and her heart.

Could she give all of herself to a man she'd known only for two weeks? And a cowboy for cripes sake. A man who represented everything she'd thought she'd left behind long ago.

Jess moved the head of his cock to the opening of Trace's core, causing her to gasp as it sent electric thrills of anticipation zinging through her. His sculpted biceps bulged, the veins along his muscles standing out like he was holding himself back with all he had. "So what's it going to be?"

Trace took a deep breath, drawing in the strength to do what she needed to do. To say what she knew needed to be said. She ran her tongue along her lower lip, and the only thing that came out was, "Okay."

His eyes flared with satisfaction. He cupped the back of her head and gently forced her to look down to where his erection was poised to enter her pussy. Her whole body vibrated as her gaze locked on his cock, so close to sliding in... So close to turning her life down another road — that road she knew she'd been approaching since the moment she'd met the man who'd become a wildcard in her future.

"Watch me take you," he demanded, his deep voice rumbling through her like a freight train barreling toward its final destination.

Blood rushed in her ears and her body was so highly sensitized that she didn't know what would happen when he finally drove home.

Home.

Jess.

She didn't have time to think anymore as Jess rammed his hips hard against her, thrusting his thick cock deep inside her pussy, *taking her*, just as he'd promised.

Trace shrieked. The orgasm that rocked her body was so fast, so unexpected that it robbed her of her breath, of all thought.

"You're *mine*." He clenched her ponytail and brought her mouth to meet his, hard and demanding, while he pressed himself against her, his cock stretching and filling her like nothing she'd ever imagined. The kiss made the waves of her orgasm continue, her core contracting around the length of him.

Omigod. Unbelievable. She'd never had an orgasm during intercourse before, and for a moment she wondered if this mind-bending climax would ever end.

Trace bit at his lower lip as she kissed him back, struggling against the jacket that still kept her arms pinned to her sides. Jess's masculine scent surrounded her, filled her senses. Their sweat mingled, their breathing hot and labored and sounding as one.

He tore his mouth from hers, kissing her chin and the length of her jaw, abrading her skin with his coarse stubble. "You feel so good wrapped around me like this."

"Take off the rest of my clothes," Trace begged, trying to free herself and frustrated that she couldn't. "I've got to touch you. I've go to."

"All right." His gaze raked over her breasts jutting from above the cups of her bra. "I know exactly what I want you to do with your hands."

Even as Jess stripped her jacket, t-shirt, and bra from her body and tossed them aside, he kept their bodies locked together. His every slightest movement pressed against a pleasure button deep within her.

When she was completely naked, Trace rubbed her palms over his hard muscled chest. "Fuck me, Jess." Her fingers trailed down to where they were joined and she slid them over the part of his shaft that was showing and was slick with her juices. "I need it wild." Her gaze met his and she was so breathless she could barely speak. "I need it *hard*."

"Hang on." His smile was absolutely sinful. "I aim to do just that." He reached up with both hands and freed her hair from the ponytail holder and tossed the band aside. "Yeah...that's better," he said while he raked his fingers through the long strands. She shivered as he let it slide over her shoulders in a sensual caress.

He eased her down so that her back was flat against the desk's polished surface. Then hooking his arms under her knees, he drew her wider apart, allowing himself to penetrate her even deeper.

Slowly he started thrusting and Trace arched her hips up to meet him. "Faster," she demanded.

"Lick your nipples while I fuck you." Jess's strokes increased, and Trace could hardly think with the sensations of pure pleasure flooding her body. "That turned me on when I watched you in the hot tub."

Jess's eyes were shadowed beneath his Stetson as he ordered her to touch herself. It made him look even darker and sexier and more dangerous than ever.

She caught her breasts in her hands and pushed them up as high as she could. It only took a slight rise of her head to flick her tongue over her nipples.

Oh, God, but it felt good...Jess driving in and out, his balls slapping her ass, her own tongue hot against her sensitive nipples, the feel of his chaps rubbing along the inside of her thighs as he fucked her, and the cool, smooth wood of the desk at her back.

She'd never experienced anything so erotic in all her life.

Clenching his jaw, Jess forced himself to keep from coming too soon. The sight of Trace spread out before him and her tongue flicking out over her nipples—*damn.* He'd never been so close to losing control.

Even though she wanted more, he'd been fighting back the desire to let all hell break loose and fuck her so hard she'd be sore for at least a month. But he'd held back, afraid to chafe her delicate thighs with his chaps, afraid to bruise the soft skin of her pussy and her ass.

"Harder!" she demanded between licks.

"You want a hard fucking," he said in a near roar, "a hard fucking is what you're gonna get."

Jess drove into her like he was hellbent for leather. Trace cried out, her eyes rolling back and she paused in what she'd been doing. "Yes, Jess. Yes!"

"Keep sucking your nipples," he ordered. "Don't stop 'til I tell you to."

She obeyed, pushing her breasts together so that she could swipe her tongue over each nipple even faster.

He focused on her jade eyes as he felt her channel start to contract around his cock. "I'm coming," she raised her head and said almost in wonder as her body trembled and her face flushed a light shade of rose. "Oh, God. I'm coming *again*."

Her words nearly pushed him over the edge, but he held back, determined to give Trace all the pleasure she deserved. The sound of her purring moans and hard slap of flesh filled the room. "Come for me," he demanded. "Right now."

A scream tore from Trace, so loud it was a wonder the barn didn't fall down around them. Her body jerked and she twisted, like she was riding a bronc. Jess thrust twice, maybe three times more, as her channel contracted around his cock. With a hoarse shout he came, shooting his come into her with hard jerks of his hips against hers. He pumped his cock in and out of her pussy, stretching out her climax and his.

When the last fragment of his orgasm settled deep in his loins, Jess eased Trace's legs down from where he'd been holding them. She wrapped her thighs tight around his hips and locked her ankles behind him, keeping him snug in her. "You're not going anywhere, cowboy," she murmured, her face flushed with satisfaction and her eyes heavy-lidded.

"Hell, no." He rubbed up against her pussy his cock growing rigid inside her in a Texas minute. "I've got plans to wear you out and then some."

Trace smiled and wiggled her hips. "I like that plan."

Bracing his hands on the smooth surface of the desk, Jess worked hard to bring his breathing down to a normal level and to control the rawness of his emotions. He'd sure as hell had gone after Trace from the moment he'd spotted her at Nicole's Christmas party. But he'd never expected to feel like a lovesick schoolboy with a crush on the hot new teacher.

Yeah, he'd known he had to have Trace. And somewhere in the back of his mind he'd known that he intended to keep her. But he'd never allowed himself to acknowledge that he might fall for her so hard.

Damn.

Trace's breathing was still rough, causing her chest to rise and fall and her breasts to jiggle. Her tempting dark rose nipples bobbed up and down, drawing his attention and luring him in to taste them for himself.

Jess took Trace's hands, intertwined their fingers together and raised them above her head. He held her there while he nipped, licked, and sucked at the tight nubs that were still wet from her own tongue. He tasted the flavor of her mouth on her nipples, mixed with the salt of her skin. Her peaches and cream scent was stronger in the valley between her breasts, a perfect blend of smells when combined with the intoxicating scent of her pussy juices.

Yep. He had it good and he had it bad.

Shards of sensation sliced through Trace as Jess bit at her nipples, and incredibly enough she felt another climax building within her. But then he pulled his cock out of her pussy and released her hands, and she whimpered in disappointment.

"I'm going to turn you over and fuck you from behind," he said, even as he rolled her onto her belly.

"God, yes," Trace said, ready for him to thrust into her pussy again. The desk felt warm and smooth against her belly and breasts, and the floor was cool beneath her bare feet. Deliciously wanton feelings surged through her as she splayed her thighs, exposing everything to Jess's eyes, and being unable to see him at the same time.

"You've got one hell of a sexy ass." His calloused palms massaged her butt cheeks as he spoke. "I love these dimples right here." She felt the brush of his lips against the small of her back and she shivered. "And here."

"Come on, Jess." Trace wiggled her rear, arching herself up to him. "Stop teasing me."

His fingers parted her butt cheeks, making her feel even more sensual, more exposed. "You ready to be fucked in the ass?"

Her heart pounded so hard she swore she could feel it against the desktop. The thought of Jess sliding into her other passage felt forbidden, and all the more exciting. She licked her lips and arched up to him. "Oh, yeah."

Satisfaction surged through him at how she trusted him enough to take him anyway he wanted to give it to her. "Hang on for the ride." Jess rubbed his cock against her slick folds, coating it in the combination of her juices and his come.

On the desktop he spotted a bottle of lotion and reached for it, then squirted it on his hand. The stuff smelled like vanilla but was thick and creamy. Perfect for sliding into her ass.

Trace made that sweet little purring sound as he used his fingers to spread lotion around the hole of her ass. He squeezed more of the lotion onto his palm and then greased his cock with it.

"I'm big and it's gonna be tight." He eased two fingers into her and she gasped. "Think you can handle me?" he asked as he reached around her with his other hand and found her clit.

"Yeah." Excitement sounded in her tone, fueling his own, and she rocked back and forth against his hands. "Definitely."

Jess grunted with satisfaction as he withdrew his fingers from her ass. He placed the head of his cock against her tight hole and gently pushed inside the opening, slowly stretching her as he entered inch by inch. "How's that?"

"Different. Wild." A moan slipped from her lips as he slid further inside. "I love how you feel."

When he was buried inside Trace, Jess gripped her hips with his free hand and started moving in and out in a slow, methodical motion. "I could fuck you all day and all night." With his other hand he continued to fondle her clit, drawing juices up and over the slippery nub. He circled it with his finger, gentle teasing strokes as he slowly fucked her ass. "I'll never get enough of you."

"Come on. More." Trace squirmed against Jess's hand and his hips as he slid in and out of her. Although she'd been curious, she'd never imagined that anal sex could feel so fine. Jess Lawless could fuck her any way he wanted and she'd take him — and she'd enjoy ever minute of it.

"Is this what you want?" His strokes increased, his leather chaps rubbing against her butt. His fingers worked her clit in a way that felt so good she could hardly stand it.

"No." Trace thrust her hips back to meet him, best she could do the way she was sprawled out on the desk, her breasts smashed flat and hurting so good. "Give me more," she insisted. She gripped the edges of the desk, holding on tight. Placing her cheek against the smooth surface she closed her eyes, the smells of lemon oil, vanilla-scented lotion, and sex filling her senses.

She reveled in the sensations of him fucking her ass. Enjoyed how he demanded more of her.

And she wanted to give it to him. Wanted to give him everything he asked for and more.

"Is that good enough for you, sugar?" he asked as he pummeled into her.

"Yes, Jess," Trace practically shouted, unable to hold back. "Oh, my God, that's it! Keep fucking my ass…ooh, just like that."

The tight coil of her climax expanded outward, larger and larger yet, growing beyond anything she'd experienced before. A different kind of climax that built to a wild frenzy of unbelievable excitement until it exploded within her.

Trace cried out and her eyelids flew open as the orgasm rocked her.

She realized two crucial pieces of information at once.

They hadn't used a condom when he'd fucked her pussy.

And her sister was standing in the doorway to the office.

Chapter Eleven

As Jess thrust his cock in and out of Trace's ass, Dee was frozen, her jaw practically hanging to the floor, and her hand clasped so tight around her heart pendant that her knuckles were white. But the moment after Trace opened her eyes and her gaze met her sister's, Dee's face turned as red as a hibiscus bloom and in a flash she backed out the door, closing it quietly behind her.

"Yeah, that's it," Jess was saying to Trace as Dee slipped out of the office. "I want you to come again."

In that moment, Trace couldn't decide whether the heat rushing through her in tandem with her climax was from sheer embarrassment...or that she was incredibly turned on because she and Jess had been watched while they fucked. She had a strong feeling that Dee had been standing there long enough to get one heck of a good show.

A sense of *déjà vu* sent goose bumps rippling along Trace's skin as she thought about those moments she'd had her own wild performances to observe — a decade ago.

Another orgasm rolled through Trace's body while Jess pounded into her. It magnified as she recalled the times when she used to sneak after Jake and Dee and watch them fuck, back when the lovers first met. From a cave near their hideaway, Trace would spy on them as she slid her hand into her jeans and fingered her clit, while her other hand pushed up under her shirt and bra to pinch her nipples.

At the same time she'd bite her lower lip to make sure she didn't let a sound escape when she came. She could still picture Dee on her hands and knees on a picnic blanket. Jake holding his cock with one hand, then guiding himself forward to thrust into Dee's pussy. Watching those two together had made her hungry for sex, but she'd never found a partner who'd matched the intensity she'd seen in her sister and Jake.

Until Jess.

An even more powerful climax whooshed through Trace as Jess took her where she'd never gone before. She rocked so hard against the desk that her mound and thighs were probably bruised. But she didn't want it to end. She wanted more.

"You feel like heaven on earth, woman." Jess's cock was as hard as steel, hard enough that he was sure he could thrust into his woman forever.

He had almost paused when from under the brim of his Stetson he'd seen Dee open the door, catching him fucking her younger sister. But when Trace hadn't said anything, and Dee had just continued standing there like she was hypnotized, Jess hadn't been able to stop.

Hell, if the boss lady got off on seeing Trace and him going at it, let her watch. Jess had caught Dee giving Jake a blow job not that long ago, so maybe turnabout was fair play. They were all grown-ups, after all.

Jess focused on the beautiful woman that he was driving into. Damn but he loved how she took him. "Your ass is so tight. Everything about you feels good."

"Oh, God. *Omigod!*" Trace cried out again with yet another climax.

His balls drew up, tightening in a rush, and then his orgasm sped through him like a bull out of a rodeo chute. He bellowed as he came, shooting semen into Trace's ass. Every part of his body throbbed in time with his pulsating cock, adrenalin rushing through him and making him feel so high that he was positive that sex with Trace was some new kind of aphrodisiac.

From the corner of his sex-fogged brain, Jess suddenly realized he'd screwed up big time. Holding back a groan, he rested his forehead between Trace's shoulder blades.

He'd just done something he'd never done before. From the time his dad had taken him to that whorehouse in Reno and Jess had lost his cherry to the well-worn brunette, he'd always used protection. *Always.*

But this time, with the one woman who really mattered to him, he'd forgotten to use a condom.

Trace sighed with pleasure as Jess braced his hands to either side of her, pressing his chest to her back. Her core continued to contract from her multiple orgasms, and his cock still felt fine right where it was.

"I'm sorry," he murmured near her ear and he kissed her softly. She could feel the sweat running down his face and chest and mingling with her own.

"Why?" Trace wriggled her hips and she swore she felt him harden inside her ass. "That was better than I'd imagined."

"I didn't protect you." Jess sighed and eased his cock out. "I forgot to use a condom."

"Yeah…that makes two of us." Trace grabbed a handful of tissues from the box on the shelf above the desk, and handed them to Jess when she turned to face him. "Forgetting protection was as much my fault as it was yours."

Instead of cleaning himself first, Jess picked up Trace by her waist and set her on the desk. "It was my job," he muttered as he pressed her thighs apart and gently started wiping the flood of juices and come from her pussy. "I've never lost my head like that before. I promised to protect you, and I screwed up."

"I went kind of crazy, too." Trace smiled and took off his Stetson so that she could see his face as he swiped at her folds with the tissues. "Just don't give me any of that 'I'll do the right thing' bullshit," she added as she put his hat onto her own head. The Stetson was so big it slipped down over her eyes, blocking her view of him.

"Hey." Jess stopped cleaning her and pushed up the brim of the hat with one hand, while moving between her thighs at the same time. He tossed the tissues onto the desk behind Trace, then caught her chin in his hand and forced her to look into his eyes. "I thought I made it clear I don't intend to let you go."

An almost shy smile curved the corner of his mouth as he added, "If we just made a baby together, I'll be the proudest daddy there ever was. You got that?"

An amazing array of feelings swirled through Trace as she stared up at her man. She barely knew him, yet she felt like they were interlocking pieces that fit perfectly together.

And *wow*, the way he was looking at her, the way he talked about having a baby together...*omigod*.

Jeez. What had one of her first thoughts been when she'd met this man?

Can I have your baby, too?

Trace reached up and wrapped her arms around Jess's neck while pulling his head down until his lips met hers. Their kiss was slow and sensuous as they tasted one another as if for the first time. Gentle strokes of their tongues and light nips with their teeth.

When they finally pulled apart, Trace slid her hands into Jess's thick brown hair. "You have hat hair." She gave him a teasing grin while she fluffed a few sweaty strands. "And cowboy forehead," she added as she observed his face was grimy from a day working the ranch, but his forehead was free of dirt from where his hat had rested.

Jess returned her grin and brushed away a streak of dirt on her cheek. "I'd say we could both use a shower."

Easing her hands through the light sprinkling of hair on his muscular chest, Trace nodded her agreement. "I'll bet we can come up with some interesting ways to get each other squeaky clean."

"I do like the way you think." He chuckled and reached across her to grab a few more tissues out of the box. His hard biceps brushed her nipples and her pussy tingled from the contact.

He straightened and wiped her juices and his come from his now semi-erect but still impressively sized member. "There's something you probably ought to know."

Jess's remark barely registered as she watched him handling his cock. The sight of his thick length in his own hand was something she found unbelievably arousing and she could already imagine him sliding into her again.

His voice lowered. "Your sister walked in on us."

"M-hmm," she murmured. But then as she realized what he'd said and her gaze shot up to meet his. "You saw Dee?"

He raised a brow as he tossed the rest of the spent tissues onto the desk. "Out of the corner of my eye."

Trace reached for Jess's chaps and pulled him closer between her thighs, needing to feel him next to her. "This is sure going to make things awkward."

That sexy smile of his about turned her to mush as he settled his hands at her waist. "Not a thing wrong with what we're doing."

When Trace nodded, his hat slipped back down over her eyes and Jess had to grin. She looked so sexy in nothing but his Stetson that it was all he could do to hold back from taking her again, *right now.*

She pushed the hat back up and he could see her green gaze. "I—I used to spy on Dee and Jake." Color rose in her cheeks as spoke. "Back when they first dated."

"You watched your sister and Jake fuck?" Now that was interesting.

Trace waved one hand toward the east. "Up in those mountains, behind the ranch, there's a sort of secret place that Dee and Jake called their hideaway. I found a cave nearby and I used to hide in there. I learned a whole lot about sex watching those two."

"Oh, yeah?" He grinned at the image of his woman watching another couple having sex. "Anyone else know about that cave?"

"No." Trace shrugged. "It's very well hidden. I always wondered if it was manmade—like some miners had dug there for gold or silver."

Jess's instincts went on high alert even as his cock ached at the thought of his woman watching her sister and boyfriend. A secret place and a cave? Might be worth investigating...in more ways than one.

"Did Jake and Dee know about this cave?"

She shook her head. "They were too busy fucking to ever go exploring."

So, likely Reynolds wouldn't have a clue it was there. Trace was probably the only one who could show it to him.

Keeping his focus on his woman—not to mention his cock that had come to full attention at the images in his mind, Jess murmured, "Did you masturbate while they fucked?"

Trace's face went so red that the light dusting of freckles across her nose stood out like copper sprinkles. She nodded and he swooped down to kiss her, hard.

"Hell," he murmured as he pulled back, his erection jutting up toward her pussy. "You've always been a hot little thing, haven't you?"

"Yeah," she whispered against his lips. "But I've never been so horny like I am around you. I want you again. Right now."

Jess released her to slide his fingers into his front pocket and pulled out one of the three condoms he'd stashed there.

Her gaze met his, surprise in her eyes. "You carry those things around with you when you're working the ranch?"

"You bet your pretty ass." He gave a slow nod. "Every day since that night at the hot tub."

"Real good answer, cowboy." She took the package from him and tore it open. "*Real* good answer."

Anticipation and excitement skittered through Trace as she rolled the condom down Jess's huge erection. When she released him, he moved the head of his cock to the opening to her core, and in one quick, hard stroke he buried himself inside her pussy.

She moaned as she dug her fingernails into his biceps and wiggled her hips. "God that feels good."

"Grab onto me and hang on," Jess said as he slid his hands under her ass.

Trace's pulse doubled as she obeyed and he easily picked her up off the desk, their bodies fused together. She wrapped her legs around his waist and clung to him. His torso was rock hard against her chest and belly, and his chaps and jeans were rough against the sensitive flesh of her ass and thighs.

Jess's gaze locked with hers as he used his powerful muscles to move her along his length. "You've got to take me to that cave," he said as he rammed her up and down his erection.

Trace had a hard time forming a coherent thought, so exquisite was the feel of him riding her on his cock like she weighed next to nothing. With every thrust he hit that pleasure center deep inside her, and it was about to send her over the edge. "You want to see where I used to watch Dee and Jake?" she asked, her words coming out in rough gasps.

"Oh, yeah." His voice was hard yet filled with sensuality. "You and I might just make some memories of our own there."

Trace gave in completely to the sensations of him fucking her while he was standing. He lowered his head and grasped one of her nipples between his teeth, and she moaned. When she tilted her head back and arched her breasts toward him, begging for more, his Stetson tumbled off her head and onto the desk behind her.

She'd had so many orgasms, Trace didn't think she'd be able to come again so quickly. But in only moments she shot toward the peak and screamed as she toppled right on over the summit.

Jess followed her moments later. As his cock pulsed inside her pussy, she rested her head against his chest. He held her close and murmured, "I'm never letting you go, sugar. You can count on that."

By the time Jess and Trace had dressed and left the barn, it was well past dinnertime and warm yellow light glowed through the curtains of the ranch house. Trace had stalled as much as possible, enjoying every moment of their time together, not wanting to leave her cowboy stud.

A sense of belonging—feelings of being wanted and of being *home*—surged through Trace when Jess draped his arm around her shoulders as they headed toward the house. The night was still, the gentle lowing of cattle floating from the corrals along with a horse's whinny in the distance. Her steps slowed when they approached the front porch, and she wished the two of them could just take off and spend time somewhere, anywhere alone.

What would it be like to wake up in Jess's strong arms? To feel his big body wrapped around hers?

"Sure you don't want me to go in with you?" The low rumble of Jess's voice tickled her ear, bringing her back to the moment and to the cowboy at her side.

Trace shook her head and felt his lips brush over her hair. "I think I'd rather face my sister alone and get it over with."

He squeezed her tighter to him while they walked up the front porch steps and said, "No regrets."

When they came to a stop on the porch, Trace tilted her head back and smiled up at Jess. "The only regret I have is that we didn't lock the door."

"I was too anxious to get inside you." The corner of his mouth quirked and his words made her knees weak. "And now I can't wait to get you back into my bed."

Trace slid her arms around his neck and reached up to brush her lips along his jaw line. "We didn't exactly make it into bed, you know." Smells of their sex and sweat filled her senses, making her pussy ache and her nipples tighten. Where Jess was concerned she was insatiable.

He gave a soft chuckle as he settled his palms on her hips. "No, we sure didn't." Sliding his hands lower, he cupped her ass and squeezed. "But we sure as hell had some fun."

Trace purred as Jess pressed his hips against hers and she felt the hard line of his cock. He was just as insatiable as she was. She felt sore and well ridden in all locations, and yet she couldn't wait to saddle up that cowboy and take him out for another hard ride.

He gave her a soft lingering kiss that left her breathless and wanting more. It took all her strength to force herself to break away from him. "I—I'd better get inside."

Jess raised his hand to her ear and skimmed his knuckles along the row of gold earrings. "Sure you don't want me to come?"

Oh, she wanted him all right. And she could think of lots of ways for him to come.

Instead she caught his hand in hers and pressed it close to her cheek. He opened his hand and she turned to press her lips against his palm and flicked her tongue against the calloused skin.

Jess's fingers shot into her hair and he dragged her to him for a bruising kiss. He bit at her lower lip, just hard enough to cause her to cry out in surprise.

"Damn, woman," he muttered when he finally released her. "I'm tempted to haul you off and fuck you again."

Oh, my.

Trace's knees wobbled as she backed away. "I'll meet you at eleven for our ride up to the cave. In front of Dancer's stall." She opened the front door with one hand, her eyes still fixed on Jess as she slipped into the house. Just before she shut the door, she gave him a sultry smile and said, "I'll bring lunch. You bring the condoms."

Chapter Twelve

Holding her breath, as if that might help her slip inside without being noticed, Trace shut the door quietly behind her. Yes, she needed to face her sister and get it over with, but first she'd like to shower and change. She smelled like sweat and sex and barn dust, and she knew she looked like hell.

Of course Dee *had* just seen her with Jess's cock in her ass.

She released her breath and rolled her eyes to the ceiling. Jeez. At least when she had spied on Dee and Jake, they'd never caught her.

Pausing for a moment, she listened for sounds from the kitchen and heard nothing. After she quietly kicked her shoes off at the front door, Trace walked as silently as possible through the living room. The tile felt cool beneath her sock covered feet as she stole down the hallway and passed Dee's and Jake's closed bedroom door.

She slipped away into her own bedroom, locked the door behind her, then stripped off her soiled clothing and tossed it all into the hamper in the adjoining bathroom. While she ran the shower until the room filled with steam, memories of her wild evening with Jess continued to scroll through her mind.

Cripes.

No doubt she was becoming some kind of sex fiend. That's all she'd been able to think about from the moment she'd met Jess. Not to mention that tonight she'd gotten off by knowing Dee had watched them.

Water pelted Trace's skin as she climbed into the shower, the warmth chasing away the sweat of exercise and sex. From head to toe her muscles had the pleasant ache of being well fucked, her nipples and pussy tender. Even her ass felt different—like she missed Jess's cock there, too.

The comforting smell of her peach scented shampoo filled her senses as she squirted a generous dollop into her hand and then washed her hair. When she rinsed it out, streams of lather flowed over her sensitized breasts and nipples, down her flat belly and over her mound. Traveling over her like Jess's hands had.

She hadn't been entirely honest with him about wanting to face Dee alone. Once she was away from the heat of the moment, away from her need to have Jess's cock inside and his arms around her, fear had started to replace the desire. She needed space away from him, needed time to think about the future, her career, *everything*.

What if she was pregnant? She definitely wasn't ready to be a mother. Jess claimed he wasn't about to let her go, but was that what she wanted?

He was a cowboy for goodness sake. What would they do? Live here on the ranch and raise a passel of kids? Not that he'd asked her to marry him, but what if he did...would she be expected to be a good little ranch wife who cooked dinner for her man?

Okay, so that was a bit stereotypical. Trace had to smile at her own generalization. She knew plenty of women ranchers, like her own sister, who ran an entire ranch operation on their own, or side-by-side with their men. Heck, on the other side of the mountain she knew of two women who ran their ranch together, as partners in *every* way. Renee Duarte and Shannon Hanes had one of the most profitable operations in the county.

Closing her eyes, Trace turned her face to the water, letting it splash over her forehead and down her face. She'd worked so hard to get to where she was with Wildgames. Four years of busting her ass, working countless hours to rise to the top, and she was *this* close to being offered the position of Public Relations Director. After that, a few years down the road, she could be the next Vice President of PR.

She'd already made one monumental decision and had walked away from the caring man she'd dated for the past two years. Tossed that relationship right out the door after less than two weeks of knowing Jess Lawless. She'd left security and her comfortable world and headed straight into the wilds and the unknown.

What, am I insane?

With a groan Trace opened her eyes, grabbed the luffa sponge and squirted peaches and cream-scented shower gel on the pad. As she scrubbed her body, thoughts of Jess tried to push aside her doubts and fears. Memories of how he'd touched her, how he'd filled her.

Was sex enough?

Yet it wasn't just sex that attracted her to Jess, or the way he looked at her and made her feel as though she was the most important thing in the world to him. She'd watched him interact with the other ranch hands, observed his leadership and fairness. And even though he'd been mad as hell at the arsonist, she'd seen the concern in his eyes for her and her sister the night the barn was set on fire.

But was that enough to make a relationship work? And was it worth leaving everything that she'd worked so hard for?

No matter how she tried to fight it, though, Trace knew she was falling in love with one cowboy named Jess Lawless. What she was going to do about it...at this moment she didn't have a clue.

* * * * *

After Jess walked Trace to the front door of the ranch house, he headed straight to his cabin. If his quarters weren't so close to the bunkhouse where the half-dozen ranch hands lived, Jess would have hauled Trace out here with him and kept her all night long.

'Course the night wasn't over yet.

When he faded into the darkness, out of sight from the house, Jess stopped and quickly retrieved the small firearm from the top of his boot. Even though he couldn't stop thinking about his woman, he wasn't so far gone that he would fail to ensure his building and surroundings were secure.

With practiced skill he listened for any unusual sounds, but all he heard was the faint creak of his leather chaps and the light brush of his boots over dirt as he continued toward his cabin and up to the front door.

As he checked to make sure his cabin hadn't been entered since he'd left that morning, an impression in the dirt by his doorstep caught his trained eye. After a quick glance around, his senses on full alert, he examined the print.

Easily 'bout the size of a woman's booted foot, but a little smaller than Trace's or Dee's, he'd wager. He frowned as he dug his key out of his front pocket and checked the thin strip of paper he'd lodged between the door and the frame, close to the threshold. Still there, so likely no one had been in his place. Who the hell had been snooping around his cabin, and why?

After he'd done a quick sweep of the apartment and locked the door, Jess yanked his cell phone out of his pocket and dialed his partner.

"Santiago," the man answered after one ring.

"Lawless here." Jess ambled into the kitchenette as he spoke. "Got a lead I'm gonna check out tomorrow. In the mountains behind the MacLeod Ranch."

"Yeah?" Santiago said over the whinny of a horse. The man must be doing some field work.

With his free hand, Jess yanked open the fridge and grabbed the carton of milk. "Gotta gut feeling we're getting close." He slammed the carton onto the counter and let the fridge close behind him.

The cell phone crackled, and he barely heard Santiago ask, "What'd you step into this time?"

Jess reached into the cabinet over the microwave, snagged the Wheaties, and set the box beside the milk. "Arson. Poisoned cattle."

Santiago let out a low whistle. "Stomping on some toes, eh?"

"Could be." Jess located a small mixing bowl before searching for a clean spoon, then realized they were all in the dishwasher that he'd forgotten to start.

"Where're you headed?"

Silverware rattled as Jess looked in a drawer for something to use and found a serving spoon. Good as anything. "A civilian is leading me out to the location—apparently she's the only one who knows where it is. I want to make sure I'm covered, but I've got to keep it under wraps." He popped the Wheaties top and ripped open the bag inside. "I don't want to take a chance on anything happening to her."

Santiago chuckled. "Been going deep undercover with this one, eh?"

Jess gritted his teeth and shook the Wheaties so hard that half the box emptied into and around the bowl. "Just stay close to the Flying M. Keep your cell on."

"Gotcha. Watch your ass out there."

"Yep." Jess punched off the cell phone and stuffed it into his pocket.

If it wasn't for that boot print he'd noticed outside his door, he'd have felt a hell of a lot better. Who could have been sniffing around?

As he dumped a liberal amount of sugar onto his flakes, Jess considered what he'd have to do tomorrow. Somehow he'd have to let Trace know he wasn't who she thought he was. He wondered how she'd take it when she found out that he was an undercover agent for the DEA.

* * * * *

When she'd finished taking her shower, combed out her wet hair, and had stalled as long as possible, Trace yanked on a comfortable pair of flannel pajamas and slippers and headed to the kitchen. It was close to ten but she had a good feeling she'd find Dee there.

Trace's stomach growled as she padded down the hallway—she hadn't eaten since noon and she was starving. She passed the twinkling Christmas tree, rounded the corner and headed into the kitchen, and sure enough, there was Dee at the breakfast nook with a half gallon of Rocky Road and two spoons sticking out of the ice cream. Her sister appeared to be deep in thought, playing with her spoon in the Rocky Road.

The kitchen was spotless, but Trace caught the delicious smell of roasted meat—probably pot roast—and her stomach grumbled again. It was so quiet that the rumbling of her belly was the only sound Trace could hear other than the ticking of the kitchen clock.

As she approached her sister, Trace felt heat rise to her face. "Save any for me?" she asked as she sank into the chair opposite of Dee.

Dee looked up and smiled as she gestured toward one of the spoons. "Dig in. Unless you'd rather start with dinner."

Thankful to have something to do with her hands and mouth, Trace shook her head and grasped the spoon. "This is most definitely the dinner of champions," she replied as she dug out a particularly large chunk and then stuffed it into her mouth.

"So..." Dee's voice trailed off, and Trace knew what was coming next. "You and Jess, huh?"

Trace shrugged, her face burning hotter than ever while she studied her spoon and slowly chewed the chocolate ice cream filled with marshmallows, nuts and fudge. The taste was welcoming and comforting, and somehow it had always made it easier to talk with her sister.

After she swallowed, Trace glanced from her spoon to her sister. "It all started that first night I came home. I met Jess at Nicole's Christmas party."

Dee raised one eyebrow. "You've been seeing him for the past two weeks?"

"Well, sort of, but not exactly." Trace dug her spoon into the softening ice cream. "He's been working on me, and I've been fighting the attraction," she said before taking another bite.

Shaking her head Dee replied, "That sounds awfully familiar." She winked at Trace. "And knowing Jess, when he sets his mind to something, he doesn't give up. Not for anything." She licked her spoon, a thoughtful look on her face. "So what about Herman?"

Trace swallowed the mouthful of Rocky Road and snorted back a laugh. "Harold."

"Whatever." Dee pushed the ice cream carton aside and leaned over the table, closer to Trace. "Neither suits him. Just that accent alone's enough to give any woman the shivers. And he's one *fine* looking man. When he came up to the house looking for you, it was all I could do to find my tongue."

With a smile, Trace replied, "I sure fell for that refined British accent." Her smile faded as she considered the reason why their relationship hadn't worked. "I really think the world of Harold, but the problem was that he was *too* reserved. I know he cares about me, and probably loves me in his own way, but something happened in his past that caused him to lock away his emotions and feelings."

Trace toyed with the spoon as she spoke, studying her upside down reflection on its shiny surface. "It wasn't until I met Jess that I realized Harold was truly passionless. I realized that I need someone who's able to feel and *live*." She raised her eyes to meet her sister's. "And I wasn't the right woman to set him free."

"Sorry about walking in on you and Jess." Dee's cheeks went pink and her hand moved to the peridot heart pendant at her throat. "I was feeding the horses and that devil Imp, when I heard noises in the office."

"We should have locked the door." Trace was sure her own face was Christmas red. "It was our first time, and we went kind of wild."

Dee's eyebrows shot up. "Your first time with him and he gave it to you in the ass?"

Resisting the urge to duck under the table and hide, Trace nodded. "Well, actually, that was after we did it the, ah, usual way."

Her sister leaned forward on the table again. "So tell me. How did it feel? In the ass, I mean."

Trace laughed and before she thought better of it, she said, "As wild as you and Jake have always had it, you've never tried anal sex?"

Dee frowned. "I've never told you about our sex life."

"Oops." Trace chewed the inside of her lower lip, then decided to spill the beans. "You know, back when you and Jake were dating...before he left?"

Dee's spoon clattered to the tabletop and she clasped her pendant tighter. "You didn't."

Trace hid a grin and gave a solemn nod instead. "Up at that place you called your hideaway. There's a cave hidden behind some bushes. I was curious and hid out there and watched you guys."

"Oh. My. God." Dee slowly shook her head, an expression of disbelief on her features. "I can't believe it."

"Let's just say it was a real education for a seventeen-year-old girl." Trace stuck her spoon into the ice cream that had softened to the point of turning into a mudslide instead of Rocky Road. "Better eat up. It's melting."

Laughter escaped Dee and she raised her hands in an I-give-up gesture. "Well, I sure don't feel so bad walking in on you and Jess now."

Trace snorted and giggled and then in the next moment the sisters collapsed into fits of laughter. Tears rolled down their cheeks, and Trace laughed so hard that her stomach ached.

God, but it felt good to laugh.

And it felt real good to be home.

Chapter Thirteen

Dressed in a comfy pair of old blue jeans, a jade-green t-shirt, Nikes, and a jacket to keep out the chill, Trace hurried from the ranch house toward the barn to meet up with Jess. She'd French-braided her hair to keep it out of her face and had kept her makeup light. After all, she was hoping he'd be kissing off all her lipstick anyway.

Flutters stirred in her belly in anticipation of seeing Jess. She shrugged the lunch bag higher on her shoulder and entered the dark recesses of the barn. The acrid smell of smoke left over from the fire still surprised her every time she entered the barn, reminding her that their little world wasn't as safe as she'd always thought it to be. Things like that happened to other people, but since she'd been back at the ranch, she'd learned that over the past few months they'd been happening just a little too often to suit all the ranchers and other folks in the area.

As she walked past Imp's stall, she caught the sound of Jess's voice at the same moment she saw him ahead, standing next to Dancer's stall. The mare was already saddled up, and Tequila, Jess's sorrel mount, was right beside Dancer.

Trace's pulse rate picked up and those flutters in her belly magnified. Lord, oh lord, he looked good wearing his black duster, black Stetson, jeans and boots. Dark and dangerous looking, that was her man.

"…be careful," Jess was saying into a cell phone as she got closer. "Just stay back…" He caught sight of Trace as she drew closer. She saw a flicker of something in his eyes, and then he gave her a brief smile and a nod as he listened to whoever it was on the other end.

"Uh-huh," he said into the phone, his gaze focused on Trace. "Gotta head on out," he added and then took the phone away from his ear and punched it off before stuffing it into his duster pocket.

Trace wanted to ask who he'd been on the phone with, but she knew it was none of her business. Instead she placed her palms on her hips and gave him a teasing look. "Cowboys and cell phones...somehow that just seems *wrong*."

With one finger, Jess beckoned to Trace to come closer. "I'll tell you what's wrong, sugar." When she reached him, his eyelids lowered as he settled his hands at her waist and brought her hips flush with his. "Waking up in the morning without you in my bed where you belong... that's a serious problem in my book."

The lunch bag fell to the dirt floor of the barn as Trace sucked in her breath. She moved her palms to his chest, feeling the tenseness in his muscles through his denim shirt. "Well, Lawless, I think I know just how to solve that problem."

Jess's blue eyes flashed with sensual fire as he lowered his mouth to claim hers, and he sank his teeth into her lower lip. Trace moaned into his mouth, and then took him deep as he thrust his tongue inside. He tightened his grip on her, rubbing his erect cock against her belly at the same time.

Her pussy grew wet and her nipples ached as she tasted his unique flavor. His masculine smell, spicy aftershave, and the clean scent of soap wrapped around her. She couldn't think...she could only feel as he kissed her absolutely senseless.

When Jess drew away, Trace was so dazed that she just stared up at him. He gave her that sexy grin of his that brought out the dimple in his cheek.

"Office," she said. "You. Me. *Now.*"

He grinned down at her. "We'd do just that if Jake and Dee weren't already in there. Doing office work, no doubt."

With a sigh, Trace replied, "If it's anything like our version of office work, they'll be in there all day."

Jess chuckled softly as he captured her mouth in another searing kiss. Trace was so hot for him that she was ready to take him in a stall and have her way with him, no matter that someone might come by.

Hot breath blew across her cheek and a soft muzzle nudged the two of them apart. Trace laughed and rubbed the nose of her black mare, Dancer. "You looking for some attention, old girl?"

"I don't know about her, but I sure am." Jess tweaked the end of Trace's braid. "Let's head on out. Maybe we'll find ourselves someplace a little more private."

The ride into the mountains behind the Flying M was a form of torture, Jess decided. While he rode Tequila, the slow and easy gait of the roan mare only added to his sexual discomfort. He swore he caught Trace's peaches and cream scent over the smell of horses and piñon, and could hear her heartbeat over the creak of saddle leather and the sound of hooves against dirt and stone.

His lawman's senses remained on high alert, always on the look out for danger. These mountains had been used for decades to smuggle not only drugs and other contraband, but illegal immigrants as well. He needed Trace to show him that cave, but he wasn't taking a chance on anything happening to her. Could be this lead would turn out to be nothing, but he had to be sure.

While their horses traveled higher into the mountain, Jess rested his hands on the saddle pommel as he studied Trace. An Arizona December breeze stirred the tendrils of hair that had escaped her braid. Her cheeks were flushed and her jacket was open, and he could see her nipples poking against the t-shirt that matched the jade of her eyes... Eyes that were so full of passion it was all he could do not to stop the horses and take her now. Hell, if it wasn't so chilly and she was wearing something a little less constraining, he'd have fucked her on horseback.

Jess's cock throbbed against the tight denim of his jeans and he shifted in his saddle.

"Not much farther," Trace said, answering his question before he asked it.

"Good thing." He gave her a smoldering look. "I don't know how much longer I'll last before I have to have my hands on you."

Her eyes widened and she ran her tongue along her lower lip. "I can't wait to get my mouth on you."

Jess clenched his reins in his fists. "All right. Your teasing's gone far enough."

Trace laughed. "Hold your horses, cowboy. It's just around that piñon tree."

"Wait a sec." Jess reached out and grabbed Dancer's halter and brought both horses to a stop. "Let me go on ahead and check it out first."

"Why?" Trace gave him a puzzled look. "I've been there dozens of times. Dee and Jake still go there, too."

"Things have changed." Jess swung one leg over his mare and dismounted, his black duster swirling around his legs. "Never know what's in these mountains these days." With a firm look, he added, "Sit tight and stay with the horses. I'll be right back."

She frowned and folded her arms across her chest, but didn't argue as Jess let Tequila's reins drop to the ground. The mare was well trained and would wait for him until he returned or until he gave the piercing whistle that was Tequila's signal to come at a gallop.

On silent booted feet, Jess moved through the trees until he came upon the secluded area surrounded by oak and piñon trees. From higher in the canyon a small stream tumbled over the rocks and down through a small ravine.

At first glance the place seemed empty. Bushes rustled to his right and in a flash he withdrew the gun from beneath his shirt, hidden at the small of his back. He trained the bead at the bush, but a second later a jackrabbit bolted out and sped across the clearing.

As far as he could tell, the area was secure. Now where the hell could that cave be—

The snap of a twig sounded behind him. Jess whirled, gun in his hand, only to point it directly at Trace.

Her face whitened at the sight of his firearm and he quickly lowered it and tucked it back under his black duster. "I told you to stay with the horses."

Trace swallowed, a confusing range of emotions swirling through her. What the hell was going on here? "I—I knew there was no way you'd find the cave without me."

His features were hard and his voice cut right through her. "It's not a good idea to sneak up on a man like that."

"I didn't know you were carrying a gun." She shifted her feet, feeling for all the world like she wanted to run but didn't have any idea why she felt that way. "Why would you need to bring one?"

"Rattlesnakes."

Trace frowned. "It's winter."

"There are a lot of different types of rattlesnakes out there." He scrubbed his hand over his face and his tone softened. "Why don't you show me that cave."

"Okaaaaay." She forced down the niggling of irritation as she skirted the clearing, not bothering to see if Jess was following her. For a big man he sure walked quietly. Pebbles and dirt crunched under her shoes, but she heard nothing from him. She was tempted to turn around to see that he was behind her, but she didn't have to — she could *feel* his presence.

When she got to the back of the clearing, she started climbing up the boulders, higher into the canyon and to the right of the stream. Her jacket protected her arms as she shrugged by spindly trees and scrawny bushes on her way up the hidden path.

Flashes of memories came back to her, memories of watching Jake and Dee fuck down below. She'd had such a perfect view. It had turned her on, making her want to experience wild and exciting sex like those two had shared. Trace never had...until she met Jess.

Watching Trace's pretty little ass as she climbed up the rocky incline was giving Jess a screaming hard-on. He kept close on her tail, but fell back a bit when she reached a ledge above the clearing. "Let me go in first," he called to her, but in the next moment she vanished.

His gut clenched and he rushed ahead to reach the ledge in a few strides. At first glance he saw only another boulder that easily topped seven feet in height. But when he rounded the boulder, he was suddenly in the cave, and Trace was waiting for him with her arms folded across her chest.

With trained precision, he quickly scanned the cave and his eyes and senses told him it was clear as far as humans or animals were concerned. To his surprise it was big enough for him to stand up in, even with his Stetson on. The floor was littered with leaves and a coating of fine dirt, and cobwebs clung to the ceiling. No sign of recent occupation by bats, wildcats, or bears.

He walked to the back of the cave and saw that it wasn't too deep and there wasn't any more to it than met the eye. Jess's muscles relaxed and he blew out his breath. He wasn't sure what he'd been expecting, but whatever it was, it wasn't here.

"Satisfied?" Trace asked from behind him. He turned to look and she had one eyebrow raised. "I'd say there's more to you than you've let on."

Jess closed the distance between them and caught her by the shoulders. "What if there is, Trace MacLeod?"

For one second she wished he wasn't touching her, wasn't so close. Her brain always seemed to go on standby when he was near, and her libido on overdrive.

The hell with it.

Trace threw her arms around his neck and pulled him to her. Jess groaned as she bit at his lip, her hunger for him driving her on in a flurry of touching, sensation, and feeling. He pushed open her jacket and shoved up her shirt and then his big palms found her naked breasts beneath.

Trace's hands reached under his duster for his shirt and she ripped the snaps apart with one tug. While he fondled her nipples, she went for his belt buckle. Their mouths never parted, their kiss wild and frantic as she undid his belt and zipped down his pants.

She tore away from him, her breathing so ragged that for a moment she was afraid she'd hyperventilate. "I want you in my mouth, Jess."

"Whoa, sugar," he murmured as she dropped to her knees on the dirt covered floor and pulled out his cock. "I need to—" he started, but then sucked in his breath as she went down on him.

His hand clenched her braid as she slid him in all the way to the back of her throat. She stroked him in time with the movements of her head, her hand sliding down to the tight curls at the base of his cock and up to the thick tip. His masculine scent exhilarated her, made her anxious to please him, to taste him.

"That's good...so fucking good." Jess's hand gripped her hair tighter, moving her more forcefully along his cock. She loved how she made him want her so badly he became even more masterful, more demanding, yet giving her everything at the same time.

Her shirt was still pushed up above her breasts and the cave's cool air brushed her nipples and caused them to ache beyond the point of pain. She brought her free hand to first one nipple, then the other, pinching and rolling each between her thumb and forefinger as she sucked and stroked his cock.

Jess groaned out loud, the sensation of Trace's mouth and hand on him sending all rational thought straight out of his head. And all irrational thought straight down to his other head. The feel of her hot, wet mouth sliding up and down his cock, that soft purring sound she made when she was turned on, the way she watched him as she sucked, and the way she tugged at each of her dark nipples in her excitement...*damn.*

"I'm gonna come," he said as he watched himself thrust in and out of her mouth. "Do you want to swallow?"

Trace purred and sucked even harder on his cock. He choked back a cry as his hips bucked against her face and his semen shot down her throat. She kept on working him 'til he had to grab her head with both hands and say, "Hold on."

With a satisfied smile, she allowed his spent member to slide out of her mouth and slowly licked her lips. "Mmmmm," she murmured. "We'll definitely have to do that again."

From zero to fully functional, Jess's cock shot back to attention. He gestured with one hand for her to stand up. The moment she was to her feet, he helped her pull off her jacket and yank her t-shirt over her head, tossing them both to the cave floor.

"Yeah, that's more like it," he said. "Now kick off your shoes."

No questions asked, Trace obeyed. Her eyes and her face, though, were fevered with her excitement, her eagerness for him.

He yanked down her jeans and she stepped out of them in a hurry, leaving her in only her socks and nothing else. She looked so beautiful with her jade eyes almost black with passion, her strawberry blonde hair sticking out of the braid, her nipples dark and swollen, and her tempting slit just waiting for him.

He'd given it to her hard last time and he'd wanted to take it nice and slow, but right now all he could think about was driving into her until she screamed out with her climax.

"Fuck me, Jess," she demanded, and that was all it took.

"Grab hold," he said even as he cupped her ass, raised her up and impaled her slick core with his cock.

"Yes!" she shouted as she gripped his shoulders, wrapped her legs around his waist beneath his duster, and arched her back. "God, you're just perfect."

Jess lifted her up and down on his cock, her bare ass rubbing against his jeans every time he buried himself deep inside her.

Harder and harder he rammed Trace, and she only begged for more. He'd never in his life been so crazy, so frantic — so in love with a woman like this.

Trace's cry tore through the cave as her pussy contracted around his cock. Jess thrust again and again and again, and she shuddered and rode out every wave of her orgasm.

Sweat poured down his face, down his chest, and down his abs, to the place where they were joined. A burst of sensation exploded in his loins and he came inside Trace in a heated rush.

Trace collapsed against his shoulder, her breathing harsh and warm upon his skin. He held her tight, keeping his cock firmly within his woman as it continued to throb and pulse.

Shit. They'd done it again—no condom. Damn, but this woman made him crazy.

"Jess," Trace said against his shoulder, her voice husky and filled with passion. "I think I'm falling in love with you."

In the next instant he heard an all too familiar click, and he froze as ice chilled his spine. Jess pressed Trace tight to him, shielding her with his body.

Laughter came from behind them and then a voice said, "At least you got that out of your system, honey...before you have to die."

Chapter Fourteen

Fuck. Jess's gut clenched as Trace gasped and stiffened in his arms. His cock was still lodged inside her pussy, she was completely naked and vulnerable...

And there was a gun-wielding bitch with her sites trained on them.

He turned his head and focused his gaze on Kathy Newman while protecting Trace the best he could with his body. "We're a little busy here," he said, trying to stall for time as he formulated a plan to get him and Trace out of this mess he'd gotten them into.

Trace peeked over his shoulder, her eyes wide. "Kathy?" Her gaze rested on the slim semi-automatic in Newman's grip, and Trace audibly caught her breath. "What's going on?"

Big Tits smiled and rested one shoulder against the cave wall, her grip never wavering. "You already know I'm an expert marksman. No doubt you realize in two shots you'll both be dead."

Jess didn't waste words. Instead he sized Newman up...the unwavering confidence in her eyes, the egotistical curve of her mouth, and her relaxed stance.

"Why?" Trace asked, and before he could stop her, she eased her legs from around his waist. His cock slid out of her core as she stood in his embrace.

"I rather liked you in that position." Newman aimed her gun at Trace's temple. "Make another move like that and you'll be one dead little slut."

Forcing his arms to relax around Trace, Jess said, "Let Trace grab her clothes and leave. This isn't about her."

"Oh, sure. Like *that's* going to happen." The woman grinned, and she actually looked like she was having a little fun.

Egotistical bitch thought this all was a game. Well, he sure as hell could use that to his advantage.

Newman's gaze lingered for a moment on his cock and her tongue flicked against her lower lip. "Nice firearm you've got there." Her cold gray eyes moved to Trace. "What a waste, firing your bullets in *that* hole. I came 'round your place last night, to show you what a real woman could offer, but you weren't home. Pity. I sure wanted a good fuck before I had to kill you."

Jess ground his teeth as he clenched Trace's arm tighter and felt her tremble beneath his hand. He didn't know whether it was from cold, embarrassment, or anger, but figured it was probably a little of everything.

"Toss me your weapon." Newman turned her gun on Jess. "The one you keep under your duster. And you know the old cliché…nice and slow, cowboy."

Jess released Trace and started to ease his right hand towards his back.

"Uh-uh." Big Tits shook her head. "I've had several pairs of eyes on you these last couple of weeks and I know you're right handed." She indicated Trace with a nod. "Hold onto the slut's arm with your shooting hand, where I can see it. Use your left to bring out the gun."

Jess tensed at her reference to his woman, but obliged and gripped Trace's arm with his right hand. He could feel her shaking even harder, and sensed her fear and confusion.

Very slowly he moved his left hand beneath his duster. 'Course he was just as deadly a shot with his left as his right, but he wasn't about to take a chance with Trace's life. He'd have to find another way to deal with this bitch.

Newman pointed her gun toward Trace's head again. "You know she's dead if you make me the tiniest bit suspicious."

"Wouldn't dream of it," he said as he slid one finger along the cell phone in his holster and pressed button number one…all in the same motion it took to move his hand to the butt of his gun.

Keeping his movements as slow as possible, Jess brought out the gun and held it up where the woman could see it, barrel pointing down. "What do you want with my gun, Newman?"

She indicated the cave opening with a jerk of her head. "Throw it all the way up there."

Jess tossed his weapon. It clattered, spun, and came to an abrupt stop at the boulder that guarded the entrance.

Her eyes never left his. "How does it feel to be left alone and defenseless with your cock hanging out, Agent Lawless?"

God damn it. How far would she take this?

Trace gasped as she stared at Kathy, unable to believe what the woman had just said. "Agent?" she repeated as she looked to Jess and almost reflexively started to step away from him.

"Don't move," he commanded her, tightening his grip on her arm.

Newman giggled and propped one hand on her hip, her nails bright red against her jeans and her pale gray eyes filled with mirth. "Sorry to spoil those feelings of love, *sugar*." She gestured at Jess with her gun. "Got a little insider info of my own that told me all about what's really going on. This slick cowboy's been fucking you for information and to get closer to that whore sister of yours. Dee MacLeod's been one of his prime suspects from day one in a little matter of drug smuggling."

Trace had felt cold and vulnerable as she'd stood there in only her socks and looking down the barrel of the gun. But now the slow heat of anger and confusion crept through her, melting away the frost.

She couldn't for a moment believe that Jess had been using her. It wasn't possible.

"You lying bitch." Trace clenched her fists as she glared at Kathy.

"Go on." Kathy smiled at Jess and gave an encouraging nod. "Tell her that you're an undercover intelligence agent with the DEA and that you hired on to the Flying M to investigate Dee."

Trace's gaze shot to meet his. "Jess?" she whispered, feeling like she was caught up in the middle of a kaleidoscope...her whole world seemed to turn upside down and every which way with only a few words, and nothing was what she thought it was. "Are you—is this...true?"

The grip he had on her upper arm lessened and he rubbed his thumb along the soft flesh of her inner elbow, as though to comfort her. "I am with the DEA, and yes, your sister was part of the investigation, but—"

She jerked her arm away. "You used me?"

"Damn it." He scowled. "No—"

"Shut up," Kathy shouted loud enough to cut through his denial, her voice echoing throughout the cave. "Time to get you two down to where the action is. You're both going to be my saving grace, so to speak. Savage and Jake are far too close, just like you, Jess. Hell, even Rick's got the pieces and he's trying to put them together. We need a smokescreen fast, so thanks for coming way up here. Now I can solve two problems at once."

Jess gave Trace a measured look, as though that was meant to clear up all the lies. If there wasn't a gun trained on them right now, she'd have socked him in the gut, like she'd done in the barn, but this time she'd make sure it would hurt like hell.

He turned away from Trace, every possible scenario running through his mind as he fixed his gaze on Kathy. "Let's see…Trace and I are going to have a lover's quarrel. I'll have supposedly shot her with my weapon and then turned my gun on myself. That'll keep everybody stirred up and distracted while you shut down this pipeline and move the operation elsewhere."

Kathy's lips tightened and her smile seemed forced. "My, what a smart special agent you are."

A muscle twitched along his jaw line. "Not very original, Newman."

"Whatever." The woman gave a bored look and braced her shooting arm with her opposite hand. Looked like she might be tiring a bit. "With the extra groundwork I've laid and doing it all here, on the MacLeod ranch—

well, that gives me some advantages, too. It'll be a big help when the feds think they've found the pipeline and the bitch responsible. That way, they won't come looking for us any time soon."

"You're gonna try to make it look like Dee was running your drug operation all along," Jess said like it was cold fact. "Then you'll quietly wait until everything dies down and open up shop."

Smile broadening, Kathy replied, "Something like that."

"Your family has money." Jess narrowed his gaze. "What the hell are you running drugs for?"

"Oh, get real." Kathy rolled her eyes, but then focused on Jess in a flash. "You know as much as I do, there's never enough to go 'round."

"And like father, like daughter," Jess said quietly.

"You leave my daddy out of this." Newman's hand trembled, the gun wavered slightly and Jess knew he'd struck a nerve.

"Henry Newman retired." Jess took advantage of her distracted anger and stuffed his cock back in his jeans as he spoke and zipped them up. He knew now she wasn't planning to shoot them until she got them to another location. Jess would be too big a body to drag far, and she couldn't afford an evidence trail that close to the cave. Not yet anyway. "Henry turned over the family business to his little girl," Jess continued, "and she's trying to make it as big as Daddy did."

Anger turned Kathy's face an odd shade of purple. "I've made this operation bigger than he ever dreamed. Hell, my men are smuggling double the drugs from Mexico, and security is ten times tougher these days."

"And you're in tight with the Mexican drug cartel." Jess fastened his belt and dropped his hands to his sides. "Bet Daddy's proud."

Trace folded her arms across her naked breasts and stared at Newman, an incredulous look on her face. "How do you intend to pin your drug smuggling on Dee?"

"Well, you see..." Kathy's expression was like a wicked little girl who always got her way. "Dee MacLeod will be getting an urgent message from her kid sister to meet her right away. Near here, of course." Sighing, as though with great pleasure, Kathy continued, "Your sister will find both of your very dead bodies about the same time the sheriff's department arrives to investigate an anonymous tip."

Trace's thoughts spun and she hugged herself tighter, her body shivering as she grew even more numb from the cold. "So...you were the one who sent the post card," she said, her voice harsh. "To...to frame my sister?"

"You got that right." Kathy grinned. "All part of the plan. It'll help back up the 'evidence' showing that she double-crossed her partners."

The woman's giggle was really getting annoying. Her voice was almost singsong as she went on, "The sheriff and deputies will find not only bodies, but plenty of drugs and meticulous records that show Dee's been running this operation for the past two years. Motive, opportunity—it'll be a slam-dunk."

"They'll never buy it," Jess said. "You're wasting your time."

"I've bought the best forgery in the country. So good, in fact, that Dee MacLeod will be locked away for a very long time." Kathy stuck out her lower lip and shook her head. "Sad, really. Grieving in jail for her dead sister, and for her husband who will have lost his life in the line of duty, not long after."

"*Bitch*," Trace said with such venom that she was sure she was going to sprout fangs. "Before you have the chance to do anything to him, Jake will hunt you down like the snake you are. One way or another you'll pay in your own stinkin' blood if you carry this out."

Kathy eyed Trace's naked form and smirked. "Amazing. From such a fat cow to a skinny slut. What did you do, have head to toe lipo?"

Jess forced himself to remain calm and to keep from reacting to Newman's barbed tongue. His heart twisted as he saw how blue Trace's lips had become, and the red blotches on her skin. "Let Trace put on some clothes."

"I *am* getting sick of looking at that ugly body." Newman nodded toward Trace's clothing. "Go ahead, but just remember the 'no sudden moves' rule. Not that you're capable of doing anything more than screwing the ranch hands."

Trace's body wracked with shivers as she moved to put her clothes on, and Jess's gut tightened.

While Trace dressed, he asked Newman, "You planning to execute this plan alone?" He knew the answer before she gave it to him.

"Are you an idiot?" the woman replied with another roll of her eyes. "Figured an intelligence agent might actually be intelligent. Speaking of idiots..." Her gaze darted toward the entrance.

If Jess had been close enough to her, he'd have had a chance to disarm the bitch. She was getting tired, and she was definitely overconfident.

"Get your ass in here now, Ry," she shouted over her shoulder, but kept the gun steady on Trace. "You've taken long enough."

Big Tit's gaze returned to land on Trace, who had finished dressing and was crouched down, tying her Nikes. "Maybe I should just shoot you here," Newman said. "Your dead weight would be easy enough for Ry to carry."

"Forensics," Ryan Forrester said as he rounded the boulder, a pistol in his hand. "We need to do this just right and wait to kill 'em down at the stash."

Trace stood, her eyes widening at the man's appearance, but Jess didn't even blink. He'd known all along that Forrester was tied into the drug operation, he just hadn't been positive exactly who the bastard had been working for.

"Grab Lawless' gun," Newman ordered Forrester. "On the floor, to your left. Give it to me. And keep your weapon trained on Lawless. I'll watch the slut."

"Ryan Forrester." Jess made sure he said it nice and slow and loud enough to carry to the cell phone in his holster. "You've sure been one tough bastard to track down."

The man chuckled as he scooped up Jess's gun and handed it to Newman before he backed up to the cave mouth again, his own weapon trained on Jess. "After the way you fucked up my rustling operation," Forrester said, "this is gonna be sweet. Almost as sweet as screwing with Dee MacLeod and Kev Grand. My favorite smokescreens."

Where the hell is Santiago? Jess thought. His partner was supposed to have kept close by, and the GPS in Jess's phone should have led the man straight here.

"Is everything ready?" Newman asked Forrester as she tucked Jess's gun into her back pocket.

The man gave a quick nod. "And tied with a friggin' bow."

"He's that former deputy my sister mentioned," Trace said, recognition dawning in her expression. "The one who was rustling Dee's, Catie's and Kev's cattle to pay off his gambling debts."

Jess nodded. "I've been after you for quite a while," he said to Forrester. "I knew you'd gotten in deep with the Mexican drug cartel to pay off your bookies. The rustling scheme was just a way for you to keep the focus off what's really going on…big time hauls. I bet the biggest of the big is about to go down and this time *we're* the distraction."

"And Dee's the scapegoat," Trace added.

"You're both just fucking brilliant." Newman waved her gun toward the cave entrance. "Start walking. Hands up where we can see them, yadda yadda yadda."

"Too bad we won't get to finish what we started in the barn," Trace said with an odd note in her voice. Jess cut his gaze to her and she gave him a look that said, *listen to what I'm* not *saying.* "You know, what I was doing—what *we* were doing—before Harold interrupted us."

"Shut the hell up," Newman said. "We're not interested in your fuck-a-pades."

Jess wanted to tell Trace *no*, don't try it, but she had that look in her eyes that said she'd made up her mind. Without smiling, Jess winked at Trace, so that only she could see, telling her he got her message. At this point, since backup hadn't arrived, this might be their only chance.

He raised his arms, palms forward and started toward Forrester. "What I haven't quite figured out," Jess said as he passed Newman, "is why you're working for Big Tits here."

Forrester snickered and Newman scowled. "I *was* going to let Ry kill you, but I might just keep that pleasure all for myself. Maybe I'll line you up and kill you both with the same bullet. I could, you know. I'm damn good with a gun."

"Forensics," Forrester muttered.

Newman glared at him. "Shut your hole."

Heart pounding like a herd of wild horses galloping across the desert, Trace followed behind Jess, keeping enough distance between them that she'd reach Kathy about the same time he got close to the deputy.

Trace clasped her two hands together. "I love you, Jess," she shouted at the same time she swung her fists up and under Kathy's gun arm.

Kathy screamed and the weapon fired as Trace forced the woman's hand up toward the cave's ceiling. Rock shards rained down on them, landing on their heads and faces, getting in Trace's eyes. Her eyes stung as she followed her first swing with another one, this time slicing her fists against Kathy's wrists and knocking the gun from the woman's hand.

Another shot fired. Trace didn't know if it was from Kathy's gun, and she didn't stop to think about it—or the scuffling and cursing coming from the cave's entrance.

"You fucking bitch!" With a shriek, Kathy raked her nails along Trace's cheek, but Trace didn't flinch.

Years of kickboxing training and Trace went on autopilot. She landed a punch to Kathy's jaw, snapping the woman's head back. In a flash of movement, Trace positioned herself for a side kick and slammed one Nike-clad foot down on Kathy's thigh, just above her knee.

Kathy Newman screamed again and fell back against the cave wall. Her face was a sickening shade of purple her eyes glittering with fury. Her brown hair stuck up like horns, making her look like the demon she was. "You're *so* gonna die now, slut," Kathy spat as her hand shot to her back pocket where Jess's gun was.

With a powerful right jab, Trace buried her fist in Kathy's belly, her hand sinking deep into the soft flesh.

Air rushed from Kathy's lungs in a loud *whoosh*, doubling the woman over until she dropped to her knees. Trace snatched Jess's gun from Kathy's back pocket. She backed up a few steps, and just like she'd learned at the firing range, she cocked the weapon and aimed it at the bitch's head.

The way Kathy was rolling around the floor and screaming in obvious pain, though, it wasn't likely she was going to be making any moves toward Trace.

Sparing a glance toward the front of the cave, Trace saw Jess casually standing with Forrester's gun in his hand, the sites pointed at Kathy Newman, and Trace relaxed. Forrester was face-down on the cave floor, apparently out cold, his hands cuffed behind his back with Jess's belt.

Trace's gaze met Jess's and he smiled. "I love you, too, sugar."

Chapter Fifteen

The next few days passed by in a virtual blur for Trace. She'd hardly had a chance to see Jess with all that he'd had to do to wrap up his investigation, and they hadn't had a second alone. Her body ached to feel him again, to be wrapped up tight in his arms and to feel his cock inside her core.

The moment she got him to herself, she was gonna jump him. After she beat him to death for not telling her he was a DEA agent.

With a sigh, she perched on the small stool at the vanity table in her bedroom and ran a brush through her strawberry blonde waves. But she didn't even see her own reflection. Instead she couldn't help but relive the incredible sex she'd had with Jess in the cave…and then the terrifying moments that had begun when she'd still been recovering from her orgasm.

Thank God they had made it out alive.

When Jess had reached behind him for his gun, he had managed to press a button on his cell phone. It had opened a line to some kind of special set-up that notified his partner, Santiago, and gave him Jess's coordinates, along with letting him in on the conversation in the cave. Santiago had called for backup, but had gotten sidetracked when he'd run into a group of Kathy Newman's men and the illegal immigrants they'd been using as mules to smuggle cocaine into the United States from Mexico.

After Jess had secured Kathy's hands behind her back and bound her ankles with strips of material he'd torn from his denim shirt, and had done the same to Forrester, he had whipped out his cell phone and reached Santiago.

Thirty minutes later it was all over. The Sheriff's department, the DEA, Customs, Border Patrol—heck, it had seemed like everyone had arrived. Trace had been vaguely embarrassed by the thoughts of the whole world snuffling around the cave where she'd just had wild sex—and gotten interrupted, of course, by that psychopathic bitch and her henchman.

What was it, anyway, with people catching her having sex? Payback for all those times she'd watched Dee and Jake?

Trace sighed at the thought, feeling a twinge between her legs. Here it was, Christmas Eve, and she had no idea when she would get to see Jess, or where he even was right now.

Or even what she was going to do about the future.

Yesterday she'd contacted Human Resources at Wildgames and arranged to take the next six weeks off. She had rarely taken any time off over the past four years, and upper management had no problem with her taking a little sabbatical.

If things did work out for her and her cowboy...she shook her head and smiled. A *cowboy* for cripes sake, and a lawman to boot. Anyway, if she and Jess were going to make a go at their relationship, she would see about telecommuting instead of returning to England. She could fly into London for the quarterly meetings and arrange what personnel meetings she needed to conduct during those trips. The owners of Wildgames were progressive and dynamic, and she hoped they would consider her request. If not, then she'd cross that bridge when she came to it.

After all that had happened over the past couple of weeks, Trace felt as though she had come full circle. That she could finally leave behind the old insecurities and embrace the confident woman she'd become. She didn't need to prove anything with her job or position.

She just needed to be herself...and being herself was all right.

Trace sighed again as she set the brush down, grabbed her makeup compact and popped open the lid. She patted a little more foundation along the four long scratches marring her cheek, souvenirs of her encounter with Kathy Newman.

A smile of satisfaction crept across Trace's face. She'd kicked some serious butt in that cave, and it had sure felt good to let that bitch have it. No doubt, with all the evidence the various branches of law enforcement had gathered, Kathy was going to spend a very long time in prison.

After Trace finished putting on her makeup and had fastened earrings in all of her piercings, she slipped into an elegant strapless dress that she'd bought in Paris. It was a deep shade of emerald green, reached two inches above her knee, and hugged her slender figure. She felt sophisticated, sexy, and actually beautiful in it.

Too bad Jess wasn't going to see her in the dress—unless he made it to the party at the Gadsden Hotel tonight. She hadn't really felt like going without him, but she'd promised Dee.

Trace struggled for a moment with the zipper, but finally managed to get it up. The shoes she chose were a matching green, but a decent height. Not like those death-on-sticks heels Nicole had talked her into wearing at that Christmas party where Trace had met Jess.

Speaking of Christmas parties, Catie and Jarrod should be arriving soon, Trace thought as she shifted uncomfortably. The stupid thong she was wearing was too tight, sliding up her crack and into her folds. *The hell with it.*

Trace hiked her dress, peeled off the thong and tossed it aside before pulling the dress's skirt down again. Just the feel of the outfit's silky material brushing against her bare ass and pussy was enough to make her wet. And thinking about what Jess would do to her the next time they managed to get alone…

A knock sounded at the front door — probably Catie and Jarrod here to take her to Gadsden. Dee and Jake had left earlier, needing to take care of a few things before they attended the party.

Trace grabbed her handbag and headed out of her bedroom, down the hall to the living room. Her heels clicked against the tile, and she wondered why the house was so dark. She could swear she'd left the lights on in the kitchen. Only the colorful, twinkling bulbs on the Christmas tree illuminated the living room, giving it a soft holiday glow.

Trace fixed a smile on her face and yanked open the front door —

To see Jess standing there with his sexy grin and that adorable dimple. "Merry Christmas, sugar," he said in his deep, vibrant tone.

"Jess." Trace's voice was only a hoarse whisper as she threw her arms around his neck and pressed her body to his.

Their mouths met, frantic, urgent, and demanding. He yanked up her skirt and groaned with obvious satisfaction when his palms rested on her naked ass. The next thing she knew, he'd picked her up and she'd wrapped her legs around his hips. Her head spun as he swung her around and backed her against the wall, never breaking contact with their kiss.

He felt so good, smelled so good, tasted so good.

Somehow he unbuckled his belt and she felt the coarse brush of denim against her mound as he unfastened his jeans. Their hands and their mouths didn't stop moving. And when he freed his cock, he drove it immediately into her core.

Oh, God. It felt so good with Jess fucking her pussy as his tongue plunged in and out of her mouth. Hard and fast he thrust into her, hurtling her so fast toward the peak that she could barely breathe.

Trace purred her pleasure and her climax blasted through her in a flurry of incredible sensation. Jess swallowed her cries as his hips jerked against hers and his hot fluid filled her core.

Lights blazed on, sudden and blinding.

At the exact same moment several voices shouted, "Surprise!"

And then the room went completely silent.

Trace tore her mouth from Jess's and buried her face against his shirt. "Oh. My God."

"Shit," he muttered.

"Um…oops," Dee's voice came from behind them. "Ah, guys, let's head back into the kitchen. We'll break out the food while these two, uh, say hello."

Giggles, laughter, snorts, and scattered conversation faded as the crowd moved out of the living room and into the kitchen.

"Sorry," Dee said, and then the living room went dark again, leaving only the twinkling Christmas lights.

When the room was quiet, Trace tilted her head to look up at Jess. "Think we'll ever be able to have sex without someone walking in on us?"

"Maybe." Jess grinned and pressed his forehead to hers. "At least until we have kids."

As far as Jess was concerned, they didn't need to join any damn party—but that was purely for selfish reasons. He'd wanted to keep Trace all to himself. But despite her embarrassment, she'd told him that they might as well get it over with.

Somehow that sounded familiar.

While Trace had "freshened" up in her bathroom, Jess took her overnight bag out to his truck where he'd left a bag packed with a few of his own things. Once they escaped from this mandatory shindig, Jess was going to steal her away for some serious time alone.

Turned out that everything had been a set-up—other than them being caught fucking. Catie Savage had asked Jess to pick up Trace exactly at seven, to take her to the party at the Gadsden. "Something came up at the last minute," Catie had said.

Hell, something had come up all right.

When Trace was as ready as she'd ever be, she and Jess joined the party that was now in full swing.

"Nice of you to make it," Jake said with a grin as they reached the living room.

"I'm really sorry." Dee shook her head, a blush creeping up her neck as she reached for her heart pendant. "We had planned the surprise party out so well...it just never occurred to me..."

"I can assure you that we were definitely surprised," Jess said with a straight face and Jake snorted with laughter.

"What is this all about?" Trace asked, sweeping her arm to encompass the room and all the guests.

"I planned this ages ago." Dee shrugged. "It's a welcome home party. I really missed you, brat."

Trace smiled up at her older sister. "Thanks. It means a lot to me...string bean."

For the next couple of hours, Trace and Jess mingled at the party. The whole time he kept her close to his side, his arm around her waist in a protective embrace. She was grateful for his support as they talked with one person after another...all of whom had seen her with her dress hiked up to her waist and her legs around Jess's hips.

"Nice ass," Nicole said with a snicker after she and Trace hugged.

Trace gave her a mock frown. "I keep telling you to stop eyeing my ass."

With a wink, Nicole replied, "Well then, keep it covered, sweetie."

It seemed like most of their friends had made it. Of course Catie and Jarrod Savage, Steve Wilds and his girlfriend Natalie Garcia, Kev Grand, Diego Santiago, Ann O'Malley, Renee Duarte and Shannon Hanes...

And even Harold Rockmore St. John.

"Good show," Harold said with a wink at Trace and kissed her flaming hot cheek.

Great. Her ex-almost-fiancé had seen them too.

"Thanks." She reached up and brushed her lips over his cheek. "Merry Christmas, Harold."

Harold's smile turned into a frown as he focused his deep brown gaze settled on Jess. "If you hurt Tracilynn in the slightest, I shall be forced to don my old sparring gloves, and...how do you Americans say it?" Harold pursed his lips and then continued, "Oh, yes. I shall beat the shit out of you."

Trace snorted and then burst out laughing. Harold, saying *shit*? Maybe his wild side *could* be unearthed.

Jess raised an eyebrow and grinned. "You can rest easy, partner."

"Harold was called "the Rock" back in his boxing days," Trace told Jess. "During his career he won all but one of his matches."

"Is that so?" Jess looked surprised, and suitably impressed.

"Yes, well." Harold shrugged and studied his wine glass. "A long time ago."

"Rock." Ann O'Malley, a vivacious brunette, joined them, a full bottle of beer in her hand. "It suits you. Much better than Harold."

Harold's gaze lifted from his wine glass, fixed on Ann, and his nostrils flared. His expression was one that Trace had seen only a handful of times, when he was ruthlessly pursuing a future client for Wildgames.

Looked like maybe he'd just found himself a new American experiment.

Ann broke eye contact with Harold and turned to Trace and Jess. "Have a merry Christmas, you two." She gave an impish look and added, "Just try to keep your clothes on in public, okay?"

Trace groaned and rolled her eyes. "We'll never live this down."

Jess grinned and pinched Trace's ass, causing her to yelp in surprise. "Maybe we need to give them something else to talk about," he murmured close to her ear.

"My apologies," Harold said to Ann, his expression intent as he studied her and extended his hand. "I didn't catch your name."

She offered her hand in return, and when Harold clasped it, her blue eyes widened. The electric currents between them were so tangible that Trace could feel them.

"Ann O'Malley." Her gaze moved from Harold's face and slid down his lean but well muscled body. When her eyes met his again, she casually reached out and took the wine glass from his hand and replaced it with the bottle of beer she'd been holding. "Nice to meet you...Rock."

And then she turned and walked away.

Harold raised one brow, his eyes focused on the gentle sway of Ann's retreating backside. "Excuse me." He spared a quick glance for Jess and Trace. "I do believe it's time for me to move on."

Trace smiled and nodded in the direction Ann had just gone. "Hurry up. I think it's about time you found your wild side."

"Indeed," he muttered as he strode into the crowd.

"I think he's got the right idea." Jess scooped Trace up in his arms so fast her head spun.

She shrieked and grabbed onto his neck. "Jess Lawless!"

"Get a room this time," someone shouted from the crowd and everyone burst into laughter.

"You can count on that," Jess said as he strode to the front door. "This time there'll be no interruptions, and no peep show."

Chapter Sixteen

The twenty minute drive to the hotel in Douglas was twenty minutes too damn long, as far as Jess was concerned. He'd barely had the presence of mind to grab the overnight bags they'd packed from out of his truck, then the wait at the check-in and the time it took to ride up in the elevator to their room was unbearable.

They couldn't keep their hands or mouths off one another in the elevator, and if there'd been the slightest chance they could have gotten away with it, he would have fucked her right there.

But this time Jess intended to have Trace all to himself.

"Hurry," Trace demanded when he slid the card key in the lock.

The moment the door was open, Jess swept her up in his arms and kicked the door shut behind them.

He needed to be in her so bad it was all he could do not to rip that sexy little dress right off her. Trace was just as frantic. She kissed his stubbled jaw, his ear, his lips — anything she could get her mouth on while he carried her to the king-sized bed in the middle of the room.

Somehow they both ended up tumbling onto the bed, their kissing wild and frenzied. He'd wanted to make love to her slow and easy this time, but all he could think about was driving his cock inside her pussy and possessing her in every way.

Mind, body, heart, and soul.

Trace's head spun. She hadn't had any alcohol at the party, yet she felt intoxicated, drunk with her need for Jess. One of her shoes slipped off and her dress hiked up to her waist as they rolled across the bed. In the next moment she found herself on top of Jess, her thighs straddling his hips.

He'd lost his hat and his hair was a sexy mess, his eyes like blue fire as she looked down at him. "You make me crazy, woman," he said as he reached down and teased the soft hair on her mound with his thumb.

"Then at least we're crazy together." She pulled his shirt out of his jeans and ripped the snaps apart, baring his sculpted chest.

Jess's hands were just as busy as hers. He yanked down the top of her strapless dress so that she was completely exposed, save for the material bunched up around her waist.

Trace scooted down onto his thighs. Her fingers didn't even falter as she unbuckled his belt, undid his jeans, and freed his cock.

His palms were like fire as he cupped her breasts, kneading them and pinching her nipples as she wrapped her hands around his cock and rose up on her knees.

"Fuck me," Jess ordered as she placed his erection at the opening to her channel.

Coming down in a swift movement Trace impaled herself on his long, rigid length and cried out with the pleasure of feeling him so deep. And the way his cock curved slightly, it hit her g-spot, dead on. "You fit me so perfect," she said as she wiggled.

"Oh, yeah." He gripped her hips. "That's it, sugar. Now ride me hard."

Trace raised herself up so that his cock was almost out of her, than plunged back down so that his cock pressed against her pleasure button, and then she did it again and again. Her breasts bounced as she rode him, the slap of flesh and the creak of the bed frame an echo of her moans.

Jess thrust his hips up to meet her, pounding that spot that felt so unbelievably delicious deep inside. His jeans were rough against her ass and the inside of her thighs, the scrape of the denim adding to her excitement.

"I—I'm coming," Trace said as her eyes locked with Jess's. His tense jaw and his wild blue gaze somehow tightened the spiral in her abdomen, and when the power of her climax unleashed itself, she totally and completely came undone.

"Damn, that's it," she heard him say through the storm of sensation lashing through her. He shouted something she didn't understand and then his hips bucked against hers, driving his cock still deeper yet and forcing the whirlwind of her orgasm to go on and on.

His cock throbbed and pulsed inside her sensitive core and she collapsed against his chest, totally exhausted, spent, and satisfied.

Jess woke with Trace curled up on his chest and his cock still inside her—and it was hard as a steel rod. Her peaches and cream perfume blended with the smell of the rich cream between her thighs.

He craned his neck to get a better look at her face and smiled at the sight of her sleeping. That cute freckled nose, the dark crescents of her lashes against her cheeks, her smudged makeup, and her wild hair spread across her cheek and tumbling onto his chest...

She had never looked more beautiful.

Carefully he brushed the hair from her face with his fingers and tucked it behind the ear with all those glittering gold earrings. He frowned as he studied the scratches he'd just revealed along her cheek from that bitch Newman. He'd never been so terrified in all his life as he had when he'd heard that gun go off, and Trace was scuffling with Newman. But he'd been so damn proud of Trace, too, for taking that woman down the way she did.

Stirring in his arms, Trace purred, a soft smile curving the corner of her mouth. Her lashes fluttered open and then her jade green eyes met his. "Hi," she said.

Jess brushed another lock of strawberry blonde hair behind her ear. "Have we met, sugar?"

"I hope so." Trace covered her mouth with her fingers, holding back a small yawn before adding, "Otherwise a strange man has a very long and hard tool inside my pussy."

He pumped his hips a couple of times. "You mean this?"

Her eyes rolled back and she moaned. "Oh, my. Yes."

In a quick movement, Jess flipped over. Trace squealed and laughed as he pinned her beneath him and braced his arms to either side of her arms. "You ready for another round?" he asked with a small thrust of his hips.

"Whoa, cowboy." She squeezed her thighs around his waist and gave him a mock frown. "Now that we've fucked without someone walking in on us—"

"This session's not over yet," Jess cut in with a grin.

Trace laughed and went on, "Why don't we try sex with *both* of us naked. Entirely naked. As in no socks, no dress around my waist, and you with every last stitch of clothing off." She pursed her lips as she eyed him, before adding, "Well, you could wear the hat."

He chuckled. "One problem."

She raised an eyebrow. "What's that?"

"How do I get my clothes off without taking my cock out of you?"

With an unladylike snort she braced her palms against his chest and pushed at him. "Don't make me get mean with you, cowboy."

"Now that I'd like to see." He didn't budge as she giggled and kept trying to shove him off of her. "You're about as mean as a potato."

"What? Ooooh…" Trace gave him a pretty fierce look for a spud. "Just you wait."

"All right." Jess laughed and eased away and then stood beside the bed. He kicked off his boots and peeled off his socks as Trace slid her crumpled dress from around her waist and tossed it across the room.

"I was wondering," Jess said as he shoved down his jeans, "if you'd come with me to Houston tomorrow for Christmas dinner with my mom and the rest of the Lawless clan."

"I'd love to." A radiant smile spread across Trace's face. "Definitely wouldn't want you to disappoint your mother. And I'd sure love to taste some of that special pecan pie you said she makes for Christmas."

"It's the best." He gave her a quick grin. "Can't wait for Mom to meet you, sugar."

When he was naked, Jess stood beside the bed, his hungry eyes taking Trace in. She reclined on her side as she watched him. Her long hair spilled over her breasts, her nipples peeking through, and the soft hair of her mound glistening with their juices.

Damn. It took every shred of his control not to slide between those pale thighs and thrust his cock inside her and fuck her long and hard.

Whoa, Lawless. He ground his teeth. *Take it slow this time.*

Trace's heart beat a little faster as her man studied her as though she was a seven course dinner he was about to devour. Her nipples tightened and her pussy grew wetter yet. "What are you waiting for?"

He didn't answer, and she swallowed hard. Cripes but he was gorgeous—that broad chest, those well defined muscles, and lord, oh lord, but those powerful thighs...*yummy.*

Jess reached down and grabbed his overnight bag that had been dropped on the floor, and she got a fine view of his tight ass. After he dug through the bag, he tossed it back on the floor and then slid on the bed beside her. He was just inches from her, and she could feel his body heat and caught the warm smell of their sex. Both his fists were clenched, and when he opened one she saw that he had a bright red condom package on his palm.

"We seem to have a problem remembering these things," he said, his voice and expression serious.

Biting the inside of her lower lip, she glanced down at the package and then looked back to him. "You make me so crazy I can't think past wanting you inside me."

With a slow nod, he said, "Could be we've already made a baby. Then again, maybe not. But we need to decide now if we're ready to start our family."

Her eyes widened and her heart pounded faster. "We haven't even talked about our future, Jess. Much less starting a—a *family* for goodness sake."

He uncurled his other fist, and her pounding heart shot straight up to her throat and lodged itself there. A ring. A gorgeous solitaire diamond in an antique gold setting.

All along her skin goose bumps sprouted and she began to shiver. Her gaze met his again and he was smiling. "Marry me, sugar. I know we've got a lot to work out. What we're both gonna do about our careers, where we'll live…when we want to start our family. We'll work it out. Just say you'll marry me."

Trace swallowed hard, but couldn't get past that throbbing in her throat. She pushed herself to a sitting position and just stared at him.

"Of course," he added, and the corner of his mouth quirked, "asking's just a formality. Like I said before— you're mine and I'm never letting you go."

"Wow," she finally got out. "Everything you said…wow."

Amusement glittered in his wicked blue eyes. "And…"

"Yeah, I'll marry you," she told her wildcard and gave him a teasing smile. "As long as you promise to wear those chaps for me. Frequently."

"You've got yourself a deal." With a soft laugh, Jess took her left hand and slid the diamond onto her ring finger.

Sparkles flashed and glittered, and Trace sighed at the beauty of the flawless diamond. "Perfect fit."

"Your sister was a big help," Jess said as he rubbed his thumb over the back of her hand.

"Recruiting my family now, are you?"

Expression completely serious, he nodded. "Helps to have informants well positioned."

Trace laughed and then quieted when he held up the red condom package and said, "It may be too late already to have a choice in the matter. I'm ready to start a family and have a couple of kids or more. But I'd like to know how you feel about it."

"I didn't think I was." She sighed and reached out to run her fingertips down his chest. "I'm still not sure I am. I know I want to be a family with you in every way. But maybe we should use these for now, and then if I'm not pregnant I'll go on the pill until we're both ready."

"Damn but I love you." Jess ripped the package open and sheathed himself in a hurry. In the next moment he had her flat on her back and he was between her thighs.

He slid into her core and she gasped and arched up to meet him. "I love you, Jess."

Slowly Jess thrust into Trace, making love to her body, mind, heart and soul. Their pounding hearts seemed to join as one, so loud that it all but surrounded her. Their mouths mated and they swallowed one another's cries as their climaxes blended and swirled and fused into one.

As tremors wracked her body, and through the haze that shrouded her mind, Trace heard the door open, and at the same time a voice called out, "Housekeeping!"

Epilogue

Rick McAllister dragged his hand over his stubbled face as he settled into the plastic airport seat. He just wanted to get out of dreary San Francisco, back to Arizona, and home to his son.

And then catch those damn *coyotes*, the people-smugglers who'd managed to elude him far too long. Especially the bastard known as *El Torero*.

He pulled his black Stetson low so that he could observe people around him without being obvious. In his line of work as an Intelligence Agent with the U.S. Border Patrol, people-watching was a necessary skill. But now he was doing it to pass the time before his plane was scheduled to depart.

Hair at Rick's nape prickled—he had the distinct feeling *he* was being watched. He casually looked to his left to see a young woman staring at the screen of a notebook computer. Something in his gut told him she'd been studying *him* a fraction of a second earlier.

The corner of his mouth turned up. He wouldn't mind if she *had* been checking him out.

Rick pushed up the brim of his Stetson and raked his gaze over the woman. She sure was pretty, her shoulder-length hair the golden color of an Arizona sunrise. She had the type of shapely figure he preferred, nicely rounded and damn sexy. From a gap in her pink silk blouse he could see a little bit of lace covering her generous breasts, and damn if her nipples weren't pushing up against that soft material. His gaze traveled down to those long legs beneath the skirt that hit a couple of inches above her knees. Yeah, she had great legs and definitely great—

He broke off his appraisal as the woman glanced up and her gaze met his. She had gorgeous eyes, warm and deep brown—and the connection between Rick and the woman, for that fraction of time, was tangible. Like she'd done lassoed him with that one look. She immediately blushed a pretty shade of pink and looked back at her computer.

Rick couldn't help but grin. Damn, she was cute. She might be worth getting to know.

Well, hell. Wasn't it just last night he'd told his sister Callie that he didn't want a relationship? In the five years since Lorraine's death, he hadn't met a single woman he was interested in pursuing. Not one. He'd gone on dates, but few and far between, and often just in the line of work. Yet there he was, fascinated with a stranger in an airport a thousand miles from home.

"Flight 1216 with non-stop service to Tucson is now boarding rows one through twenty-five," announced a voice over the intercom.

Rick stood, and noticed the woman had slipped her laptop into a bag and was already walking toward the gate, giving him a nice view.

Yeah, she definitely had sexy legs, and damn but she had a great ass, too.

Several passengers crowded in front of Rick, so he had to wait a while longer for his turn to board. When he finally made it onto the plane, he worked his way back and noticed the pretty blonde in a window seat, staring outside. He checked the number and couldn't believe his luck—she was sitting in seat 23A and his was 23B. What were the odds of that?

He took off his Stetson and set it in the overhead compartment. With his big frame, he normally disliked sitting in the middle, but apparently that was all Callie could get him on this flight, and it was working out just fine. He eased into the seat, extended the seatbelt, and buckled it.

A flight attendant helped an elderly lady put her bag into the overhead compartment, and then the lady sat next to Rick. He nodded to her and said, "Ma'am."

The woman's pale blue eyes held a hint of amusement. "You're too polite to be a Californian."

"Just spent a week in Frisco with my sister and her twins." He smiled at the memory, wishing he'd been able to spend more time with his niece and nephew. If he hadn't had to go to that briefing in San Diego beforehand, he could've taken his son Trevor to Callie's with him. He sure missed the kid and looked forward to getting home.

"I'm visiting my grandchildren in Tucson." The lady shook her head and sighed. "Hellions, all. Love them, but a weekend is about as much as I can handle. Now those kids could use some lessons in manners."

She punctuated her statement with a jab of her fist in the air, then began digging through an enormous purse. "I have some pictures their father sent in here somewhere…"

Rick held back a grin and glanced at the woman in pink on his other side. Her forehead was pressed to the pane, and she was apparently lost in her thoughts. She sure smelled good. Real good. Like honeysuckle and soap, clean and fresh.

The windowpane felt cool against Lani Stanton's forehead as she stared into the darkness. She couldn't help thinking about her lunch with Theresa and Calinda a couple of days ago and their conversation about Lani meeting a cowboy on her trip to Arizona. She would have to tell her friends she saw a handsome specimen right there in the San Francisco airport.

And wait until she told Trace MacLeod—make that Trace Lawless now—whose idea it was for Lani to make this trip in the first place. Trace had moved back to Arizona six months ago after finding herself a sexy cowboy—and then married him.

Lani sighed and turned her thoughts back to that gorgeous hunk of man in boots she'd seen in the airport. She'd been so embarrassed to find him studying her from beneath his black cowboy hat. What incredible blue eyes he had—and that grin could melt a woman's soul. Thank goodness he hadn't noticed her watching him a minute before. As a journalist she'd become a people watcher, and lord, was that man something to watch.

Lani groaned. What was wrong with her? She had no interest in men after being married to the biggest asshole of the century. After seeing what her father had put her mother through when she was growing up, she should have known better. She should never have let James's lies make her believe in happily-ever-afters.

But as far as that cowboy, what harm was there in looking? Kind of like window shopping with no intention of sampling or buying the merchandise.

She was finally free, finally divorced from James.

Speaking of the bastard, how did he learn that she was going out of town? Last night he'd left a message on her answering machine, demanding that she call him before she left. As if she'd waste another second of her time on him.

"Good riddance, jerk," she grumbled, her breath fogging the pane.

"Beg pardon?"

Lani jumped at the sound of the husky voice, so close that a shiver sprinted down her spine. As she whirled in the cramped seat, her elbow rammed hard flesh. Heat crept up her neck when she saw the cowboy's blue eyes wince.

"I'm so sorry!" Her gaze swept over the tanned face, strong chin, and the chestnut hair that had been hidden under the cowboy hat earlier. "Did I hurt you?"

The man grabbed his side and grimaced as though in mortal pain. "I'm not sure I'll live."

He winked.

That familiar flush spread through Lani, the telltale blush that would redden her face from the roots of her hair to the tips of her toes. She offered a half smile and turned back to the window.

Lights flashed on the wing and reflected on the wet asphalt, a steady rhythm in time with her throbbing pulse. She watched as a man guided the plane onto the runway. Her heart rate rocketed, her palms slick with sweat. The scar on her leg ached and she rubbed at it through her skirt.

"I apologize if I embarrassed you," the man beside her said, his voice low and disturbingly close.

A thrill rippled through her belly as she forced herself to face the man. "Not at all."

"Rick McAllister." White teeth flashed against tan skin as he smiled and offered his hand.

Lani caught his earthy scent of sun-warmed flesh and apples, and she fought the desire to dry her moist palm on her skirt before his calloused hand engulfed hers. His grasp sent tingles through her mons and breasts, and she quickly pulled away.

"And your name, Ma'am?" he said in that slow and sexy voice that made her nipples even tighter.

"Oh." She swallowed, feeling flustered and on edge. "I'm Lani. Lani Stanton."

"Lainee," Rick drawled, a slight, almost imperceptible country twang to his voice, and she shivered. "A pretty name for a pretty lady."

Just the way he was looking at her, the way he said her name, made her want to squirm in her seat.

Good lord. If just talking to this man was making her feel like this, what would it feel like to *really* be with him?

Nope. Not going there. She'd had it with men, and that was *that*.

About the author:

Cheyenne McCray is a thirty-something wild thing at heart, with a passion for sensual romance and a happily-ever-after...but always with a twist. A University of Arizona alumnus, Chey has been writing ever since she can remember, back to her kindergarten days when she penned her first poem. She always knew that one day she would write novels, and with her love of fantasy and romance, combined with her passionate nature, erotic romance is a perfect genre for her. Cheyenne's books have won numerous awards, including "Best Erotic Novel of the Year," by the Romantic Times BOOKclub, The Road to Romance's "Reviewer's Choice Award," Romance Reviews Today's "Perfect 10 Award," and the CAPA for "Best New Author."

In addition to her adult work, Chey is also published in young adult literary fiction under another name. Chey enjoys spending time with her husband and three sons, traveling, working out at the health club, playing racquetball, and of course writing, writing, writing.

Cheyenne welcomes mail from readers. You can write to her c/o Ellora's Cave Publishing at 1056 Home Avenue, Akron OH 44310-3502.

Why an electronic book?

We live in the Information Age—an exciting time in the history of human civilization in which technology rules supreme and continues to progress in leaps and bounds every minute of every hour of every day. For a multitude of reasons, more and more avid literary fans are opting to purchase e-books instead of paperbacks. The question to those not yet initiated to the world of electronic reading is simply: *why?*

1. *Price.* An electronic title at Ellora's Cave Publishing and Cerridwen Press runs anywhere from 40-75% less than the cover price of the <u>exact same title</u> in paperback format. Why? Cold mathematics. It is less expensive to publish an e-book than it is to publish a paperback, so the savings are passed along to the consumer.

2. *Space.* Running out of room to house your paperback books? That is one worry you will never have with electronic novels. For a low one-time cost, you can purchase a handheld computer designed specifically for e-reading purposes. Many e-readers are larger than the average handheld, giving you plenty of screen room. Better yet, hundreds of titles can be stored within your new library—a single microchip. (Please note that Ellora's Cave and Cerridwen Press does not endorse any specific brands. You can check our website at www.ellorascave.com or

www.cerridwenpress.com for customer recommendations we make available to new consumers.)

3. *Mobility.* Because your new library now consists of only a microchip, your entire cache of books can be taken with you wherever you go.

4. *Personal preferences are accounted for.* Are the words you are currently reading too small? Too large? Too...**ANNOYING**? Paperback books cannot be modified according to personal preferences, but e-books can.

5. *Instant gratification.* Is it the middle of the night and all the bookstores are closed? Are you tired of waiting days—sometimes weeks—for online and offline bookstores to ship the novels you bought? Ellora's Cave Publishing sells instantaneous downloads 24 hours a day, 7 days a week, 365 days a year. Our e-book delivery system is 100% automated, meaning your order is filled as soon as you pay for it.

Those are a few of the top reasons why electronic novels are displacing paperbacks for many an avid reader. As always, Ellora's Cave and Cerridwen Press welcomes your questions and comments. We invite you to email us at service@ellorascave.com, service@cerridwenpress.com or write to us directly at: 1056 Home Ave. Akron OH 44310-3502.

NEED A MORE EXCITING WAY TO PLAN YOUR DAY?

ELLORA'S CAVEMEN

2006 CALENDAR

COMING THIS FALL

THE
ELLORA'S CAVE
LIBRARY

Stay up to date with Ellora's Cave Titles
in Print with our Quarterly Catalog.

To recieve a catalog,
send an email with your name
and mailing address to:

CATALOG@ELLORASCAVE.COM

or send a letter or postcard
with your mailing address to:
Catalog Request
c/o Ellora's Cave Publishing, Inc.
1337 Commerce Drive #13
Stow, OH 44224

Discover for yourself why readers can't get enough of the multiple award-winning publisher Ellora's Cave. Whether you prefer e-books or paperbacks, be sure to visit EC on the web at www.ellorascave.com for an erotic reading experience that will leave you breathless.

www.ellorascave.com